# The Mountain

By JoAnn Conner

To Jenny—
Enjoy the adventure
and mystery!

JoAnn Conner
October 13, 2018

Reviews for *Heartwood*    by JoAnn Conner

"Ms. Conner has done her research, so the basic historical facts are in place from which to spin her story of murder, survival and love."

- Taylor Flynn, Tahoe Mountain News

## Acknowledgements

My first thanks goes to my granddaughter, Savanna Adams, my hiking buddy, supporter, and fellow writer. It is she who showed me the spot where we took the shot for the cover of this book. She and I are also working on a book together, in the teen genre.

Thank you to all my children: my son, Matthew Adams, for the consult on guns and tools that could be used on the rocks. Thank you to my son Luke for his advice and experience in the use of the Talkabouts we used during the Angora Fire. Thank you to my daughter, Rebecca Michaud, for all her marketing efforts. Thank you to her husband, Andy, for his computer expertise. Thank you to MaryBeth for being my bookkeeper and her accounting advice.

Thank you to my editor, Dianne Rees, and to Scott Blumenthal for his input on plot development.

## Preface

Native American people roamed across the United States for centuries before the North American continent was even discovered. Their artifacts, burial grounds, and stone markings, called petroglyphs, have been found in many places in the United States. While different tribes settled in specific geographic locations, there were also those who traveled.

Modern historians and archeologists seek to find documentation for these tribes, and many of the artifacts are displayed in museums or returned to the tribes themselves, particularly in the case of human remains.

I came to appreciate and respect Native American culture even more when I was honored to work with Elders Dinah Pete and Eleanor Smokey from the Washoe Tribe, and Wanda Bachelor from the Maidu and Washoe. These people taught their ways gently, and with reverence for the old ways.

However, there will always be those who seek to turn a profit from these rare, sometimes sacred items. Because of this, I have not been specific as to the areas in this novel. I sincerely hope my readers will appreciate the story and the message.

# Chapter 1

Susanna Warren stepped out of the car and looked up at the mountain towering before her. She drew a deep breath, enjoying the fresh, clean air. Her eyes took in the clear, blue sky, the vivid evergreens, and the natural shrubs. Manzanita, with its deep red branches and green leaves, was intermingled with sage and lupine. She loved the smell of the sage; almost like honey, and especially fragrant after a rain. A Stellar Jay landed on a branch near her and tilted his head back and forth, inspecting the intruder in his domain. Susanna laughed as the Jay began to screech at her.

"Boy, have I missed this!" she said, pulling her golden brown hair back behind her neck and securing it with a pony tail band. She had been doing some graduate work helping on an archeological site on tribal land in North Dakota. But her heart was in the Sierra Nevada Mountains, where she had been raised, and when the opportunity to work close to home came up, she jumped at the chance.

Her green eyes scanned the forest in front of her, looking for the path she wanted. Snagging her pack from the backseat and checking her water bottle, she slipped it in the side pouch of her pack. The day was beautiful, but she was glad she had chosen to wear her light weight parka sweater. She locked the car, attached the keys with a clip to her belt loop, tucked the dangling keys into her pocket, and shoved her hat on her head. Taking off at a brisk pace, she started up the path, taking in the vegetation and mentally cataloging the species of trees in her beloved Tahoe.

This was ancient Washoe land, and she was hoping to be able to prove they had camped and hunted in this particular area. It was a shame that so little of the land actually belonged to the native tribe in this day and age. The Washoe used to come up to Lake Tahoe every summer, to gather pine nuts and fish. They would seek out the acorns and grind them to make a mash. The willows they used to make their baskets grew in plentiful supply near the streams and parts of the lake shore. They would spend the summer in Lake Tahoe, preparing for winter in the Carson Valley.

But, their visits to the lake slowly decreased as development increased. After a Washoe man was ticketed for fishing without a license in the 1920's, they did not come to camp much anymore. The willows were removed for stream restoration work and to build houses on the edge of the lake itself. Hunting required a license, as did fishing; both being an insult to the old ways. They found that they, who loved and cared for this great lake, and who had first shown this lake to the white man, no longer owned any land on the lake shore. Pushed into the Anglo schools, much of the Washoe language was lost as well.

There were supposedly old ovens and grinding rocks here, near some of the petroglyphs in the Truckee area. She had been on that site years ago, with her grandfather, but was looking for new evidence to justify funding a small party to map and log this area, further south from the discovery in the Truckee region. It would be wonderful to bring more artifacts back to the National Museum of the American Indian branch of the Smithsonian.

After two hours of steady ascent through the woods, Susanna walked out on an outcropping of rock and looked around. The views were stunning, and most prominently before her was a field of bright yellow Wyethia wildflowers, commonly referred to as mules ears, and beautiful, purple lupine, ending in a scattering of crystal and granite rock.

She smiled as she remembered the first time she found out the Indians used the soft leaves of the mules ears as toilet paper. Her grandfather had laughed at her expression, but when she actually touched the leaves and considered the alternative, she was impressed with the ingenuity of the Native Americans. Her grandfather. He had been the one to save her when she lost her parents at the age of four. He gave her the love of these mountains, and taught her respect for nature.

She took her compass out of her pocket to check her bearings. According to her compass, the area she needed to survey was just a half mile to the east. She was slipping the compass back into her pocket when suddenly the rock underneath her started to vibrate, followed by a muffled boom.

"That sounded like an explosion!" she said out loud. "Why would anyone be blasting up here?" Cautiously, she began to pick her way upward in the direction from which the explosion came. She walked carefully, listening intently for any sign of people or animals hurrying towards her.

Thirty minutes later she heard voices, masculine voices. Two, no three different voices. She crept closer, trying to make out what they were saying. Susanna peered around a big tree, and saw a mountain of rock; boulders that stood as if stacked, like giant, irregular blocks, and filled with petroglyphs. This is what she had been searching for! She stood, hidden behind a large Jeffrey pine, watching the men as they dug in the area under the petroglyphs. They shouldn't be disturbing this area!

"We need to get this one out of here," said one of the men. "Dig deeper, we need to get it to break free! Come on, you lazy pigs!" The voice was agitated and had an edge to it.

Susanna leaned a little more forward around the tree and saw the three men, standing next to a good sized boulder.

"This one is the biggest yet, and that guy is expecting us to deliver it by tomorrow!" The speaker was tall and of average build, although slightly stooped. He wore a blue shirt and black jeans. His hair was thinning on top, with a pronounced widow's peak, and was the color and texture of dried straw. He looked to be about fifty-five and his face was lined, like you would expect from years of too much drinking. Susanna immediately took a dislike to him.

"But Boss, "protested the second man, "this one is going to be tough to get on the truck!" He was younger, probably mid twenties, with sandy blond hair, and dressed in worn jeans with a green and black flannel shirt and work boots. "It must weigh three or four hundred pounds, easy!"

"That's what you get paid for!" snarled the older man. "Do you think I hired strong, young, dumb types to question my orders? " His face was twisted in a menacing scowl. "You can be replaced any time; I want it done today or you know I will make you sorry!" He advanced on the younger man, shaking his finger in his face, his eyes bulging with anger.

"We are short a man, Boss," began the third man, whom Susanna also guessed to be about twenty-five. His gray shirt was open to reveal a white tee shirt stained with dirt and sweat. He looked strong, with muscles straining the fabric across his chest. His black hair was mostly covered by a black and green baseball style hat. "Gary should be back any minute," he said calmly, "and the extra man power would really help."

"Did I ask you for excuses?" hissed the older man, known only as Boss, as he whirled on the third man and walked towards him until he put his face inches away from him. His eyes were almost bugged out and his mouth was twisted in a snarl.

"I'm just saying we usually have Gary to help, and this is a really heavy one," replied the young man. "I wouldn't want it to slip and break." He smiled evenly at the Boss, who stepped back and looked at him with suspicious eyes, not sure if he was being played or not.

When the older man moved, Susanna got a better look at the boulder. She could not be certain until she got a closer look, but the boulder had images scratched in its surface; images that looked very much like Washoe rock art!

Susanna shifted and slowly pulled her iPhone out of her pocket. She focused her phone to take a picture; at least she could provide evidence. She adjusted the phone and stepped forward a little to get a better view.

The crack of the small branch breaking under her boot split the quiet mountain air like a clap of thunder. For a few seconds, all four of them froze. As one, the three men turned in her direction. Then she heard it…the unmistakable racking of a shotgun off to her left!

Before she could move, strong arms suddenly wrapped

around her waist and she was lifted off the ground and swung away from the scene in front of her. The scream in her throat was muffled by a hand across her mouth and she felt herself falling as the roar of the shotgun assaulted her ears. She hit the ground with a thud, scratching and clawing at the hands confining her. She struggled against the weight of the man on top of her, pinning her to the ground.

"Be quiet!" he hissed in her ear. "We need to get out of here!" Before she could break loose, he was off her and yanking her to her feet and down the trail. Another blast of a shotgun peppered the trees to their right. She could hear shouts behind them as they ran through the forest.

They veered off through the shrubs and trees, the Manzanita ripping at her jeans. They had covered about twenty feet, when suddenly the man pulling her leapt off an embankment, dragging her with him, causing her to stifle another scream as her feet left solid ground. He turned as he landed and caught her, breaking her fall as her feet hit the soft ground five feet below, but he did not stop.

Charging across a shallow stream, he pulled her around a bend, raced across a small open space of granite rock, and dropped them both down behind a huge fallen tree. Rolling on top of her, he peered under a limb, looking back the way they came.

"Get off…" she started to say, but a big hand clamped across her mouth.

"Shhh!" he whispered, continuing to look through the broken branches. "Lay still!"

She stopped struggling and turned her head slightly to follow his gaze. She had no idea who this man was, but he had taken her away from the person who was shooting at her. She did not see or hear anything. Her eyes shifted back to study his face, trying to read his expression.

His eyes were fixed on the other side of the open rock area, his sculpted, clean shaven jaw clamped tight. A swath of brown hair fell across his forehead, almost tickling her nose, but the hair on the back of his head was closely cropped.

She was conscious of the rise and fall of his chest against her, and the pressure of his body against hers. In another time and place… she shook herself mentally, bringing her back to the present.

Who was this guy? He didn't seem to be trying to hurt her, which was an improvement over someone shooting at her. Several more minutes went by until he finally shifted his gaze to her face. She found herself looking into expressive dark brown eyes, with long dark lashes. His strong, straight nose gave a classic look to his tanned face. He looked like a man who spent time outside frequently.

"I'm not here to hurt you," he said quietly. "Those men are dangerous. If I take my hand off your mouth, will you promise not to scream?" His eyes held concern. She nodded and he moved his hand.

"You're heavy," she whispered. His face registered surprise, then broke into a smile, showing well formed teeth and full lips. He pushed his strong arms up and shifted off her.

"Sorry, M'am" he smiled. "I was trying to keep you from getting shot." He kept his voice low and soft.

"Who are you?" she whispered, not wanting to speak in a normal voice in case the other men were near and could hear them.

"Jeff" he answered quietly, "and you?"

"Susanna," she replied.

"Nice to meet you, M'am," he said, "now let's get out of here." Casting another look towards the stream, he rose to a crouching position and offered his hand to help her up. He easily pulled her to her feet. "Stay low for a little longer," he said, taking her hand again and leading her behind several deadfalls into a stand of trees.

"M'am?" she mused as he pulled her through the trees. She had no idea where she was and couldn't get to her compass while they were moving so fast. He dropped her hand, but kept watching behind them. Who is this guy? And where was he taking her? Well, at least he wasn't trying to shoot her! She decided to take her chances and followed him for over half an hour before they came to a clearing.

A dark green Jeep was parked on the edge of the clearing across from where they stood. He held his hand up to stop her as he looked carefully around the clearing. He crouched, listening intently for several minutes, and then seemed to relax.

"I think we lost them," he said, standing to his full height. She guessed him to be about six feet two inches tall. "Come on," he said as he strode across the clearing to the car. He went around to the passenger side and opened the door. He stood holding the door open and looked at her. "Get in; I'll give you a ride to your car. Where are you parked?"

"Whoa, hold on there cowboy," Susanna said, noting his western style shirt, blue jeans, and boots for the first time. She crossed her arms and stood facing him, several feet away. "Who are you? I don't know you from Adam…"

"It's Jeff," he grinned.

"Uh huh…funny guy, aren't you? Well, mister, just what were you doing out there?" He moved away from the door, and broke into a slow smile. He crossed his arms and leaned against the rear bumper of the car, with a twinkle in his eye.

"Well, "he said, "I think I was saving your life." He turned slightly and reaching into the back seat of the Jeep, took out a Stetson, which he placed on his head. "M'am," he said, touching his hand to his hat brim.

"Yeah, about that. Why were you there? How did you just happen to be there at exactly the right moment? Who are you? And what's with the cowboy hat and the 'm'am' stuff?"

"Actually, I should be asking you the same questions. What were you doing out there? Who, exactly, are you?" His gaze locked on her eyes and held them, unfazed by her resistance.

"That's really none of your business."

"Yes, actually, it is my business. Do you know those men?" He stood away from the Jeep now, his hands on his hips. "Were you out there to steal artifacts too? Did you have a deal that went bad?" She stood, speechless, her mouth gaping open. "Give me a good reason why I shouldn't arrest you?" he continued, his gaze not wavering.

"Arrest me! Steal…what? Oh that just does it! You think you are so funny!" Susanna could feel her cheeks starting to burn as her temper ignited. "I just lost my pack, my work, and nearly got killed and you crack jokes! I am so done!" She turned and started to march back in the direction she thought she left her car.

"Stop," he said, "come back here."

"Ha!" She kept walking, faster now.

"I am ordering you to stop and come back here now!" His voice had a stern quality to it now.

"Listen, John Wayne…" she retorted, still moving away.

"It's Jeff."

"Whatever! I appreciate you saving my life," she said whirling around to face him, "but I've had enough of your stupid games…." He was walking towards her, holding up a badge. "Oh, nice try, but what is that, a badge you bought at a flea market somewhere?"

He stopped in front of her, still holding the badge and staring into her eyes. He reached into his back pocket and drew out his wallet, flipping it open to reveal an ID card with him in a sheriff's uniform.

"Sheriff Jeff Clellan, at your service, M'am." She stared at him. "Now will you please come back and get in the car? I'd like to get us somewhere safer…and I do have a few questions for you."

"Sheriff?" She stood there looking into his deep brown eyes. He shifted to place his hand gently in the small of her back and started to move her towards the car.

"Now, please M'am, get in the car." His eyes scanned the brush and trees quickly while they walked the few steps to the Jeep. He held the door for her as she slid into the seat. What the heck did she wander into? Why was the Sheriff out in the woods?

"Do you have a gun?" she demanded suddenly. He was taken aback by the ferocity in her voice.

"Why?" He gave her a puzzled look.

"Do you?" she persisted.

"Are you going to try to wrestle it away from me?" One eyebrow was arched as he looked at her. What was she getting at now?

"You do!" She glared at him.

"Well...I am the Sheriff."

"Why didn't you shoot them!"

"Excuse me?"

"You let them shoot at me and you didn't try to stop them?" His face held a stunned look as he stared at her. He shook his head.

"It's not that easy," he said quietly.

"What's not easy? They shoot at me, you shoot back! It's not rocket science, Sheriff John!"

"I was busy saving your life by getting you the hell outta there!" His face was a little red. "And the name is Jeff! Or maybe you should just call me Sheriff so you remember your place!" As soon as he said it, he realized it was a mistake. He knew she would not take it as respect for the law and the man that just saved her life. He braced himself.

"My 'place'?" she screeched. "What cave did you just climb out of, Cowboy Bob?" Her hands were bunched into fists and her mouth was screwed into a snarl. "My 'place'?"

"I didn't mean it like that," he tried to explain, "I meant..."

"Oh, I know what you meant! " She was livid. Her face was red and her hands were waving madly in the air. She was sputtering, trying to get her thoughts together to blast him with all she had done to achieve 'her place' but thoughts were racing through her mind so fast she could not articulate.

"No, you don't!" he raised his own voice to be heard over hers. He leaned into the car, his face less than a foot from her face. "Your 'place' is as a civilian who has just witnessed a crime and been involved in an incident where guns were fired. And, I had to save your life and risk mine!" Susanna was stunned by the tension in his voice. "Have you ever killed anyone?" he spoke so softly, she was frightened. His mouth was set in a grim line and his eyes flashed. She was silent. His intensity overwhelmed her and she wondered if she had pushed too far.

"Have you?" he demanded. She shook her head no. "Then it would be a good idea for you to be quiet about things you don't understand." His voice had lowered and his face had set into a scowl. She had pushed too far and suspected she had brought up memories he obviously would like to forget. He shut the door as hard as he could without slamming it, then strode around the car to the driver's side.

"Buckle your seat belt," he commanded as he put the key in the ignition and started the Jeep. They drove silently for several miles on a bumpy dirt road.

Susanna glanced at him as they drove, and saw his jaw was still clenched. She focused on watching the landscape and decided they had come down the side of the mountain opposite where she left her car. Coming around a bend, they drove onto a paved road and she squinted ahead.

"I think that is my car up ahead, on the right shoulder. The blue Subaru."

"Do you have your keys or are they up the mountain in your pack?" he asked.

"No, I have them clipped to a small chain in my pocket," she answered. "I learned the hard way once when I had them in my pack and it fell over a cliff." He looked at her, frowning.

"A cliff? Do you make a habit of finding trouble?" She felt the color rise in her cheeks.

"I do my job!" She glared at him. "But I never got shot at until I ran into you." His jaw clenched again. Suddenly she looked at her car by the road.

"Hey! Slow down, that's my car!"

"I'll send a deputy back for it," he said, without looking at her. He glanced in the rear view mirror.

"What! Stop the car, I want out!" She grabbed the roll bar and reached for her seat belt clasp with one hand. He grabbed her hand and jerked it away from the seat belt, holding it firmly while keeping one hand on the steering wheel.

"Stay put!" he snapped.

"Let me out! You can't do this!" She slapped his hand away and pulled her hand free, but before she could reach the seat belt again, he swerved the Jeep to the side of the road and brought it to an abrupt halt, raising a cloud of dust around them. He grabbed her hand again, glaring at her.

"What do you think you are doing? Brilliant idea, trying to jump out of a moving car!"

"You have no right to treat me like a criminal!" she fumed.

"Stop acting like a child, I'm trying to protect you!"

"From what, your driving?" she taunted. "Nobody is shooting at me now, so what is your problem?"

"Are you always this difficult?"

"Let go of me!" she demanded.  He opened his mouth to speak, but suddenly caught himself, looked away from her, and took a deep breath. He let go of her hand and sighed. He looked straight ahead for a moment, then turned towards her.

"Look, Susanna, I'm sorry. I am worried they might have seen your car and it would not be safe for you to drive it away until we make sure they can't find you."

"Safe? What is going on?" she said, frustration showing in her voice.

"It's a long story and I need to get some information from you first."

"Like what?"

"Like, was your identification in your pack?" he asked. She swallowed hard and looked away. "It was," he said, "I can see it in your face."

"But, my car!"

"I promise I will send a deputy back for it right away and you will have it back before we are done with the paperwork." He studied her face for a few minutes. He had really nice eyes, she thought. "Now, will you please just sit still and not try to jump out of the Jeep?  Or," he grinned, "do I have to handcuff you to the roll bar?"She started to snap back at him, and then, unexpectedly, she laughed, relieving the tension. "That's nice," he said.

"What?" she asked.

"Your laugh." He was rewarded with another smile. Nice mouth, she thought.

They rode the next several minutes in a relaxed silence, until he pulled up at the station.

# Chapter 2

He is a cowboy, she mused, as she watched him jump out of the Jeep and move around to open her door. He even offered his hand to her as she stepped down. Grandpa would have loved this man, she thought, then found herself blushing at the thought.

"Are you alright," Jeff asked her, noting the sudden pink tint in her cheeks. "You look a little flushed; would you like some water?" He opened the door to the station for her.

"Yes, thank you, that would be nice," she said, grateful for the excuse for her sudden coloring.

"Hey, Sheriff," Bodie greeted them, "find anything out there?" He stopped, looking at Susanna. The look on his face said she was not what he expected the Sheriff to find. "I mean, any suspects?" He turned back to Jeff and then glanced from him to her and back again.

"She's not a suspect, Bodie," Jeff said, "at least I don't think so yet," he grinned as he walked to the water cooler against the wall.

"Now just a minute!" Susanna protested. Jeff held up a hand.

"This is one of my deputies," he said, gesturing in Bodie's direction. "Bodie, this is Susanna...?" he stopped, a question on his face.

"Warren," she finished for him, "I'm Susanna Warren," she said, extending a hand to the deputy. They shook hands and exchanged smiles.

"I just need to ask you some questions. " Jeff said to Susanna, offering her the cold cup of water. "But first, your keys please, M'am."

"But..." she started, but Jeff cut her off with an exasperated sigh.

"My deputy could hot wire your car, but it would be easier for him to get it for you if he had your keys," he said. He faced her gravely, his hand out.

"Well!" she huffed, pulling the keys out of her pocket and

removing them from the small chain that held them in her jeans. She placed them in Jeff's outstretched hand. "Be careful with my car!" He raised an eyebrow and a smirk crossed his face in response to her glare.

"It's okay," he said solemnly, "Bodie got an excellent rating in the Sheriff's Driving Academy."
She couldn't tell if he was teasing her or was serious. She stared at him with suspicion, not quite sure.

"Bodie, a couple miles up Highway 89, just before the turn off to the crystal mines, take the dirt road to the right. There is a blue Subaru on the right side of the road," Jeff said, handing Bodie the keys. "I promised this lady I would send a deputy up to bring her car back for her. Could you help me keep that promise please?" He smiled at Bodie and the deputy looked at Susanna and grinned.

"Glad to be of service, M'am," he said, touching his hat brim.

Good grief, she thought, has the whole world gone cowboy while I was away at college?

"And Bodie," said Jeff soberly, "take Marty with you and grab a Benelli and some extra shells on your way out." Bodie looked intently at Jeff, understanding what he did not vocalize. "Keep a sharp eye; we took some gun fire about a mile up the mountain from the road." He looked at Susanna, and then motioned for Bodie to step off to the side a little.

She couldn't understand what they were saying, but she could see Bodie's face, and it looked grim. At one point, they both looked at her, then turned back to talk for a few more minutes.

"Yes, sir!" Bodie said, and strode into the back of the station. He emerged a few minutes later with another deputy, both wearing Kevlar vests now, and both carrying Benelli Super Black Eagle II shotguns. Jeff nodded at them as they walked by the desk where he sat with Susanna. His eyes followed them out of the door, concern on his face. He stared after them for a few minutes, then turned his attention back to Susanna.

"Now, Miss," he looked at her, "it is Miss, correct?" He

smiled when she nodded yes. "I need some information, so first, what is your full name and address please?" She watched him as he typed the information into the computer. He wasn't going to win any typing contests, but he didn't hunt and peck either, she thought.

"Phone number?" he continued.

"I don't give out my phone number to men I just met," she said firmly. He grinned again.

"I'm not just any man, I am the Sheriff," he said, "and you just gave me your home address, which I hope you don't give to most men you have just met." His face turned serious. "The men on the mountain may have your address by now. We need as much information as possible to help keep you safe." She thought about that for a few minutes.

"Why would they want to hurt me?" she asked. "I don't understand what is going on." He considered her carefully before posing his question.

"What did you see before they started shooting?" he asked.

"What did I see?" she repeated. Her brow furrowed and her lips pursed as she thought hard. "Well, first I felt the ground move beneath my feet. Like an explosion, but that didn't make sense," she said, looking at Jeff. He nodded to encourage her.

"I hiked up the mountain further, "she said, nodding to herself while staring at the coffee mug on his desk, "and then I heard voices."

"Voices? Were they men? Women?"

"Men," she said, "three of them."

"What did they look like?" he sat up, listening intently.

"Two of them were young, maybe mid twenties, and one was older, maybe fifty-five or so. He seemed mean." She looked at him, sitting impassively. What did he expect from her? "I don't know! Maybe if I saw them again or something."

"What happened next?" he prompted.

"I somehow knew I should be quiet," she said, "so I moved slowly forward until I could see around a tree." Susanna frowned, then closed her eyes to concentrate. "The men were arguing."

"What were they saying?"

"I don't remember," she said, blowing a breath out. "Something about how the boulder with the rock art was so heavy." She rubbed her fingers across her forehead, as if trying to pull the information to the surface.

"What else do you remember?" Jeff asked, his eyes fixed on her face for any tell tale sign she was lying. He wanted to believe she had no part in what was going on, but he had been wrong before. "What else did you see?" he nudged again.

"There was a boulder with petroglyphs on it, sitting on the ground by a truck."

"Then what?" he asked evenly.

"Then," she threw her hands up in frustration, "then, you threw me to the ground!"

"To keep you from getting shot," he asserted. Susanna shrugged her shoulders and leveled her gaze at him.

Jeff leaned back in his chair and studied her for a few minutes. He rubbed his chin as he thought, then after several minutes, he leaned forward again and scrutinized her face. She shifted impatiently and opened her mouth to speak when he cut her off.

"What were you doing on the mountain?" he asked her, carefully watching her reaction. She seemed surprised at the question.

"I am an archeologist and historian," she answered. "I guess I never told you that. I am currently looking for Washoe petroglyphs here in this area. We have reason to believe there are also ancient ovens and some encampments there as well," she replied.

"Who do you work for?"

"The Native American Branch of the Smithsonian Institute," she said.

"I don't suppose you have any credentials?" he asked.

"Of course, they are in..." she stopped. "In my back pack."

She stared at him for a minute, processing her losses.

"What is the name of your boss at the Institute?" His gaze did not waiver.

"Rebecca, but you can't reach her now, she is on vacation." Susanna looked flustered. He studied her intently.

"What else was in your back pack?" he asked.

"My driver's license, bank card, and twenty dollars in cash." She sighed. "I guess I'll have to replace those." Jeff leaned forward and tapped the keys of the computer again.

"I've notified DMV of the loss of your license, but I am afraid you will have to go in to get it replaced."

"I know," she sighed. "I've done this before."

"How often have you done this?" he asked, his eyes narrowing. He looked back at the computer screen. "Huh," he said. "Apparently several times, according to DMV." His eyes locked with hers again and she felt herself flushing.

"Things happen!" she snapped.

"Uh huh," he said, not moving his eyes from her face. "Where do you bank?" he continued.

"I don't see how that is any of your business!" she protested.

"I can put in a fraud alert," he said, without changing his expression, "or, not."

"I...well...oh alright!" she said with exasperation. "Bank of the West." He was still staring at her. He tapped some more keys, then looked at her. She stared back.

"You're welcome," he said, turning his attention back to the computer.

"Thank you," she said flatly. He shifted back to her again.

"Do you have proof of employment, or any other credentials anywhere you can access quickly?"

"I have some other paperwork at my residence, "she said. "If I had my car, I'd go get it!" she shot back at him. He picked up his hat and put it on his head.

"Well. Then I guess we better take a ride." He stood, and moved forward around the desk towards the door.

"Wait a minute, you still haven't told me what is going on!" she protested.

"Let's go get that paperwork and then we will talk," he said, holding the door open for her. She started to walk through the door he held, but suddenly stopped and turned to face him, her mouth open.

"You don't trust me!" she said, anger mounting as she realized he wasn't going to give her any information.

"Not yet," he said. "After you, M'am." She fumed in silence all the way to her house.

# Chapter 3

Jeff drove his Jeep down what passed for the main road. Susanna was a little irritated that he didn't ask her for directions, but rather drove straight to her house. He pulled to the shoulder in front of a small natural wood cabin with dark green trim.

"An honest to goodness log cabin," he mused, observing the bare front yard punctuated with small flower beds and bordered in native lupine. He also noted it backed to United States Forest Service land.

Susanna jumped out of the Jeep without waiting for him and strode to the front door. She put her hand in her pocket and stopped. Her shoulders slumped, then she turned and walked across the yard. Kneeling down in front of a fake garden bunny in a bed of daffodils, she lifted it slightly and picked up a key.

"Your deputy has my house key," she said to Jeff as she walked back towards the front door. She glared at him, daring him to say anything about her hide a key spot. He said nothing, but stood very close to her as she turned the key in the lock. As she shifted her hand to the door knob, he put his hand over hers.

"Listen, Bucko, don't get any ideas," she said. A smile moved across his face for a quick second, before he took her arm with his other hand and pulled her behind him.

"Stay here." Her protest died in her throat as he fixed her with a warning look. Jeff opened the door carefully, and then stepped inside. Several minutes passed before he came back to the front door and motioned her in.

"Satisfied, Roy Rogers?" she said sarcastically as she moved inside, but then stopped in her tracks. Her eyes could not believe what they saw. "What did you do?" she demanded. She looked at him with shock, then gazed at the coffee table her Dad had made before she was born. It was overturned and one of the legs was hanging by a single screw. The couch cushions were thrown at odd angles and the lamp was on the floor.

"Oh no! That lamp was handmade just for me!" She knelt beside the lamp.

"Don't touch it, please Susanna," said Jeff.

"It was a gift when I graduated from college," she said sadly. "It was made especially for me, by my grandfather. He made it out of Jeffrey pine because that is my favorite. Now the base is cracked and it looks like the socket has been smashed along with the bulb! " She looked at the lamp sadly, and rose and continued to scan the room.

Across the living room she saw her dining room table, which she used as a desk. Her papers were strewn on the floor and scrambled across the table. "How could you!" she said to Jeff, her lower lip trembling. Her eyes held accusation and hurt.

"I didn't do this, Susanna," Jeff said softly, pointing to the sliding glass door across the room. "The door was jimmied." Susanna peered across the room, trying to comprehend. "And there is more." Her eyes widened and she abruptly turned and ran down the hall, into her bedroom.

"No!" she cried. She sank to her knees on the rug by her bed as she picked up the pieces of a shadow box that had been smashed on the floor.
Jeff watched from the doorway as she moved the pieces around, and finding a picture, clutched it to her heart, squeezing her eyes shut as if to block it all out. He knelt beside her and reached to brush a tear from her cheek, but caught himself. Susanna opened her eyes and looked at him.

"Why? Who would do this?" she whispered, her voice breaking.

He hesitated as he looked at her crushed expression, but he had to ask. "Susanna, I know this is tough, but can you tell me if anything is missing?"

"My grandfather's arrowheads," she said, "they were a gift from a tribe for which he did a lot of work. "She looked at the picture in her hand, then turned it towards Jeff. "I helped him on that project." He saw an older man with a Native American man, who was presenting him with a shadow box full of arrowheads. The little girl in the picture was a young version of Susanna. "He taught me to love the mountains and respect the Native

Americans. He was everything to me."

Jeff stayed silent and let her talk. He knew this was helpful to people who had suffered great loss. It might help him understand this woman, and he needed to understand.

"The rock is gone too," she said, looking around the room.

"Rock?" Jeff asked, a confused frown on his face. She was worried about a missing rock?

"See, in the picture." Jeff looked at the picture more closely and saw that the young Susanna was indeed holding a rock. "It is so unusual. It's a kind of pink shade with actual natural red stripes across it." She looked at him and he nodded encouragement.

"Go ahead," he said, feeling she needed to tell the story.

"I was out one day with my grandfather and some Washoe elders. I was walking through a shallow stream with one of the elders and we both suddenly stopped and looked down at the same time. We looked at each other and she told me the rock was meant to go home with me. I kept it in the corner of this shadow box." She wiped a tear away.

"Was it valuable?" Jeff asked.

"Only to me," replied Susanna, "it wasn't a precious stone or anything like that, it was just an unusual rock that had fond memories for me. Why would anyone take it?" She fixed her gaze on Jeff, as if expecting him to have an answer.

"I don't know, Susanna," he said truthfully. It did not make any sense. Susanna looked at the picture again.

"When our parents died, my grandparents brought my brother and me here to Tahoe to live with them," she continued, rocking gently now.

She shook her head slowly, back and forth, as she looked at the picture. "I was four and Sam was six. He went to school and started making friends, but I had no one around to play with." She touched the image of the man in the picture and bit her lip while tears slipped down her cheeks. "With Sam at school, it was even worse. I was so lonely and I missed my parents so much."

"My grandmother tried, but it was no use. Baking cookies reminded me too much of my Mom." She closed her eyes for a moment. "Then my grandfather started taking me out in the woods, teaching me about the different kinds of trees and plants, and he taught me about the animals. Because he worked with Native Americans, he taught me about their culture and traditions too." She drew a ragged breath, hiccupping with a half sob, half cry.

Susanna seemed to almost go into a trance, and Jeff knew he had to pull her back or he might lose her for days.

"Is there anything else? Do you keep jewelry or money here? Any other items of value? Are any of your papers missing?" asked Jeff. He wanted to bring her mind back to focus.

"I don't think so, I only have my grandmothers ring, and it is on this chain," she said, pulling it out of her shirt. "I don't keep money stashed here, just my lap top and my papers…" She looked confused for a minute, then her face set into a hard mask. "My papers. Of course, you want to see my work papers." She got to her feet and walked back towards the kitchen.

"Susanna, that is not what I meant." He followed and watched Susanna as she stepped back into the dining area. She stopped, with a puzzled look on her face.

"Where is my lap top?" she said, the look on her face turning to horror as she looked at the counter between the kitchen and the dining area. She walked rapidly over to the counter, and looked on the other side. "I leave it here, plugged in to charge, where is it?" Her face filled with panic as he watched her search through the debris and papers in the dining room, straightening as she assembled them. He knew he would take flack for letting her move things in a crime scene, but he also knew she was in mild shock and fragile at this point. Finally, she stood. Rubbing her hands over her face, she looked at him.

"Well, Sheriff, my computer, with all my notes is gone. And so are my work papers." She looked at him defiantly. "So what now, you going to arrest me?" She held her hands out in front of her, wrists together. Her chin was up and her eyes were angry and hurt, all at the same time. He studied her. She was trying to be tough, but he knew people who had their personal things stolen and their homes ransacked, felt violated, in much the same way as if they had been physically attacked. This was her home, her refuge, a place where she had felt safe. And now all that was gone.

There it was. Her hands started to shake, then her shoulders. Her hands went to cover her face and she started to sob. He took a step closer and touched her arm. She stepped forward and leaned in against his chest. He folded her into his arms and held her, letting her cry it out.

How many victims had he held like this? He understood their feelings of helplessness and disbelief that this could happen to them. He wanted to stroke her hair, but stopped himself. That was over the line. He held her loosely until she stopped crying and pushed away from him.

"I'm fine," she said defensively. She walked to the kitchen counter and started to pick up the box of tissues on the floor.

"Don't touch that!" he said sharply, eliciting a surprised response. "I'm sorry," he said gently, "we need to check for fingerprints. I just didn't have the heart to stop you before." He pulled a clean white handkerchief out of his breast pocket and offered it to her. She looked at it like she had never seen anything like it, then took it.

"Thanks," she said, wiping her nose. Jeff took his phone off his belt and made a call to the station. He still preferred his hand held phone to the shoulder mics. He monitored her as he spoke to Bodie for a few minutes, then disconnected.

"A team will be here in a few minutes. Why don't we go pack a few things for you while we wait."

"Pack?" She shook her head back and forth, confusion taking hold.

"You can't stay here tonight." It was matter of fact, no discussion.

"I'll be fine! I can't leave!"

'Susanna..."

"No! I am not leaving! They already ripped my house and things to shreds! They would have no reason to come back, they took everything they wanted!"

"No, they didn't." he said, watching her.

"What?" She did not comprehend.

"They didn't get you," Jeff said quietly. His eyes held hers, a frankness in them that sent a chill down her spine.

"That's crazy!"

"Did you get a good look at the men on the mountain? Before they started shooting?"

"What's that got to do with anything?"

"Susanna, they are committing felonies. That's what I was doing up there; looking for them." Her face was blank. "Could you describe them? Identify them if we caught them?"

"Well yeah, but..." she stopped and shook her head. "No. No, no, no, no, no! You're just trying to scare me!"

"Did they shoot at you on the mountain?"

"That was just to scare me away..." she was shaking her head back and forth as if to chase away the thought.

"No, Susanna, you are a threat to them. You can identify them, and you witnessed them committing a felony. " He let that sink in. "Last week," he thought for a moment, then deciding she needed to hear it, continued, "we found a body in a ravine a few miles from where you saw them. We think it's connected." She was speechless. "Susanna...those artifacts could be worth millions of dollars," he continued. People have been killed for less." She just stood there, as if frozen, trying to take it all in.

"I just came here to look for petroglyphs," she said, in a daze. She crossed her arms over her chest, hugging herself. An involuntary shiver shook her.

"Is there anyone I can call for you?" he asked. She shook her head.

"No. There is no one."

"Your grandfather?" he suggested, hoping he would still be alive.

"No. My parents were both only children and they were

killed in a car accident when I was four. My grandparents raised my brother and me, but my grandmother died shortly after I started college, and we lost my grandfather a year later."

"What about your brother?"

"No. He is somewhere in Afghanistan, but I don't know where. He is with special forces." She shook her head again. "There is...no one." The loneliness in her voice was palpable. Without another word, she walked around him slowly, as if in a trance, and went down the hall.

He started to follow her when he heard a car pull up. He looked out the window, saw the cruiser in front, and Bodie walking to the door. He opened the door and started giving the instructions to the officers and tech team as they filed in and went to work, taking samples, dusting for fingerprints, and logging evidence.

"Bodie," he said, signaling him to come to over to where Jeff stood.

"Yes Sir?" he asked, threading his way across the room carefully to avoid disturbing any evidence.

"Can you find me a safe house for her tonight, please?"he asked. Bodie took another look around, then nodded with understanding.

"I'll go make a few calls." He turned and walked back outside, keying the phone on his lapel.

"Thank you," Jeff said as his deputy walked away. He watched the work for a few minutes, then satisfied, went to look for Susanna.

He found her standing in the middle of her room, staring blindly at the mess. She held a toothbrush.

"Are you alright?" he asked, stepping closer. She turned to his voice and looked up at him, with eyes that did not register. He placed his hand on her arm, but there was no response. "Susanna?" The shock is hitting her, he thought. He looked around the room, and led her to a chair in the corner, the one piece of furniture still intact. He guided her to sit. Kneeling in front of her, he took her face in both his hands and brought her eyes up to meet his.

"Susanna," he said again, with more emphasis. He did not want her to go inside herself too much. Her eyes came back into focus, and she locked them on his face for a minute. Something flickered in her eyes and she suddenly reached her hands up and pushed his hands away from her face.

"I said I was fine!" she snapped, rising quickly to her feet. She shot him a look he didn't understand. "If you don't mind, I have to pack!"

Surprised, he put his hands up in a helpless motion as he rose to his feet and shook his head. She strode to the closet, and reached inside, coming out with a small bag, into which she dropped the toothbrush she was still holding.

Next, she went into the bathroom and he could hear things being dropped into the bag. He should probably stop her, but they could also probably get all the necessary evidence from other items in the house. She walked back into the bedroom and went slowly around the room, picking up a pair of jeans, a nightgown, and a tee shirt. She added two pair of socks and another tee shirt, before her eyes came to rest on his feet, then rose to his face. She walked over to him and stood in front of him, glaring.

"Do you mind?"

"What?" He didn't know what she wanted him to do. Her eyes flicked down to his feet again and then back up to his face, disgust showing in her countenance. He looked down and nearly jumped off the bras and panties lying under his boots. She made a shooing motion with her hand, urging him to back up, which he did, until he bumped into the wall.

"Thanks for corralling my underwear there, Wyatt Earp," she said, rolling her eyes. He felt his face burning as he started to speak, then bit his tongue. She bent, grabbed a few pairs, and threw them in her bag. She shook her head in disgust, then walked out the door and down the hall. He followed, feeling a mixture of frustration and anger.

"Maybe I should have let her jump out of the Jeep and

break her damn neck," he grumbled to himself.

Bodie was waiting for him outside when he reached the living room. Stepping out into the front yard, he automatically scanned to look for anything suspicious. Susanna was sitting in the porch swing at the end of the porch, clutching her bag as if it were a security blanket.

"What did you find?" he asked.

"Chris can take her tonight. She should be safe there," answered Bodie. "You are expected at any time."

"Good work, Bodie, thanks," said Jeff, clapping his deputy on the shoulder. He looked over at Susanna and then back to Bodie. "Get Randy over here to change all the locks before you leave. Tell him we appreciate the favor, and we will pay the invoice right away. I just don't like the idea of leaving her home unsecured."

"Good thinking, boss, I'll call him right now. I won't leave here until it's done and I have the keys in my hand." Bodie walked off talking into his lapel mic again.

Jeff turned and looked at Susanna. She looked so forlorn, sitting in the swing, clutching her small bag to her chest, and staring straight ahead. He was sure now that she was not a suspect, but a victim, and in danger. It was his responsibility to keep her safe. He approached her carefully, and stood in front of her. He waited a few minutes, until her eyes finally rose to meet his.

"It's time to go, Susanna," he said gently.

"No! I can't just leave my home wide open like this!" He knelt in front of her and searched her face.

"Bodie will stay until the evidence team is finished." He was trying to ease her concerns so she would at least get some rest tonight. "We have a trusted locksmith on his way over to change all the locks, and maybe add a few to the windows. Bodie will not leave until all of that is done and your home is locked up tight. He will bring the keys to me." She still looked uncertain. "The department will pay for all the work," he added.

"I don't need your charity!" she snapped. He was silent for

a minute before he replied.

"It's not charity, and it's not meant to be insulting. You witnessed something that my department is investigating, and that put you in danger. It is my…it is the responsibility of the department to do everything we can to keep you and your home safe from this point forward." He hoped making it less personal would help her accept the gesture.

A van pulled up in front of the house and a tall, red haired man got out with a small case and walked up the path to the front door.

"Hey, Randy, thank you for coming on such short notice," said Jeff.

"I knew it was important or you wouldn't have called after hours," said Randy, shaking Jeff's hand.

"Randy, this is Susanna. This is her home," said Jeff, gesturing towards Susanna. His eyes met Randy's over the top of her head and they exchanged a meaningful look.

"It's nice to meet you, M'am," said Randy stepping forward and extending his hand. She shook it without enthusiasm. "I am very sorry this has happened to you," he continued. "I promise you, I will not leave until I have made your home as secure as humanly possible." Susanna nodded in response.

"Bodie will stay until you are done," said Jeff. "You can leave any keys with him and he will get them to us. Give him the bill as well and we'll get a check to you."

"That would be great, "said Randy, "and I am not worried. I'll get you an invoice in the morning." He nodded to Susanna. "Excuse me please, so I can get started." He turned and walked into the house.

# Chapter 4

"It's been a long day, Susanna," Jeff said, as he walked over and stood in front of her. "It's time to go and get you settled."

She nodded, then rose and followed him to the Jeep. She stepped up and sat down as he held the door. As he got in the other side, she was buckling her seat belt, without a word. He started the car and slowly pulled away, noting she didn't even look at her home. He drove for several minutes, then pulled into the parking lot of a small restaurant.

"It's been a tough day," he began, "and neither of us has eaten since breakfast." He walked around and opened the door. She looked at him, still clutching the bag. "Come on, Susanna, you need to eat something," he said softly. Then he added, "bring the bag with you if you would like."

She got out of the Jeep and hesitated, then put the bag on the floor. She stared at it a moment, then picked it up again, first clutching it to her chest, then looking at the floor of the vehicle.

"Would you like me to carry it for you?" She didn't answer. "Or, we can lock it in the car," he said, understanding her indecisiveness. She sighed, then put it back on the floor. She shut the door and waited until she heard the locks click as Jeff hit the key fob.

"I'm being a baby." she said, starting to walk towards the door of the restaurant. He stopped her with a hand on her arm. He moved to stand in front of her and put a hand on each of her arms.

"Susanna. You have been knocked to the ground by a stranger, shot at, pulled through the woods at a run, thrown down on the ground again, questioned by the law, and your refuge was invaded and your home assaulted, all in one day." He held her eyes, and the expression she read in them was almost tender. "Trust me when I tell you I have seen many people go through much less and they have fallen completely apart," he continued. "You are not 'being a baby,' you are a very strong woman."

They were standing so close, she could feel the heat from his body. For a brief instant, she wondered what it would be like to simply fall into those strong arms and be held safe against his broad chest, to be protected.

Another car pulled into the parking lot, and Jeff suddenly moved her towards the entrance. They walked inside and Jeff spoke to the hostess, who seated them in a back corner of the restaurant. They had the section to themselves. A waitress appeared with menus and took their drink orders. They studied the menus for a few minutes.

"I'm really not very hungry," she said. Jeff looked at her with concern.

"I know you may not feel very hungry, but you do need to eat something. How about some soup?" he suggested. The waitress returned with their iced tea. "What is your soup today?" he asked.

"We have broccoli, potato, cheddar, and chicken rice," she said. "Are you ready or do you need more time?" Jeff looked at Susanna and she shook her head.

"I'll have the chicken rice soup please," Susanna answered. The waitress nodded and turned to Jeff.

"I'd like a hamburger, medium, with French fries and a salad on the side, ranch dressing, please," he said. The waitress gave Jeff a big smile, nodded, and took their menus.

They sat in silence while they waited for their food, but Susanna could feel Jeff's eyes on her. The food came quickly, and Jeff ate his with relish, while Susanna ate slowly and with effort. Jeff finished first and sat, waiting patiently for her to eat most of the bowl of soup before she pushed it away.

"Would you like anything else?" the waitress asked, looking from one to the other.

"Susanna?" asked Jeff. "Coffee? Dessert?" Susanna shook her head. The waitress took the check out of her pocket and laid it on the table close to Jeff. He looked at it, took some bills out of his wallet, and put them on top of the check.

"Are you ready?" he asked.

"Yes," she said. "Thank you for dinner," she mumbled, more out of habit than anything.

"You're welcome," said Jeff, with a slightly surprised look on his face. After all she had been through, she still remembered her manners. He followed her closely back through the dining room, but when they reached the door, instead of holding it for her, he pulled her off to the side of the alcove.

"Wait here," he said, reminding her it wasn't over. He stepped outside the door and quickly to the right of the entrance. He spent several minutes scanning the parking lot, then opened the door and motioned her outside. He pulled the Jeep out of the space and began to drive, away from her home.

"Where are you taking me?" she finally asked.

"Some place safe," he replied absently, scanning the rear view and side mirrors. A few minutes later, he pulled up in front of the station.

"No!" she said, "please, don't make me stay in a jail cell!" she pleaded.

"We're just changing cars," he said gently, "it's alright." He hadn't thought how she might view pulling into the station, and he felt a little pang of remorse for not thinking ahead. Jeff moved her inside the building, walked to a board where several sets of keys were hanging, and chose one. "This way," he said, leading her to the back of the main room.

They stepped out into a fenced area and he went straight to a black sedan and opened the door. Once inside, he pulled towards the fence, touched a button on the visor, and a gate opened for the car. He made a left turn, then quickly accelerated onto the street. A block later, he made a right turn, winding up a hill in a small tract of houses. He made a series of twisting turns, watching the rear view mirror constantly, then came out on another main street. He turned right on the highway, then made an abrupt right into another neighborhood. Finally satisfied they weren't being followed, he turned onto Pioneer Trail and headed out to Meyers.

"Where are you taking me?" she asked again.

"We have a retired deputy that also lets us use their home as a safe house. You'll like Chris, and you will be safe there."

"You're going to leave me with some guy I don't even know? How long do I have to stay with him?" He looked at her in amazement. He smiled and started to answer when his phone buzzed.

"Clellan," he said into the phone. He listened for several minutes. "Good to know, Bodie, keep me posted." He glanced at her. "They got a match already on one of the prints from your place, so hopefully, we can round them up and you won't have to stay too long with Chris."

"Can't you stay with me?" she asked in a small voice. Perplexed, he pulled up to a stop sign and turned to her. Her hands were clasped tightly in her lap, and her head was down, her hair falling across her face so he could not see her expression. She was frightened. Instinctively, he reached out his hand to push back her hair, then caught himself. As much as he wanted to take her in his arms and comfort her right now, she was too vulnerable. He dropped his hand lightly to her shoulder.

"Susanna." He spoke so softly it was like a caress. Slowly, she raised her head and looked at him. Her eyes were moist and looked too large for her face. She looked so alone. Damn it. "If you want me to, I'll stay," he said, wondering what in the hell he was doing.

He pulled away from the stop sign and made a few more turns, until he finally pulled onto a street where there were only two houses, one at the corner, and a two story at the end of the cul de sac.

He cruised into the drive at the end of the road and flashed the lights. The garage door slid open and he drove in and parked next to a large SUV. The garage door closed behind them and a light went on in the garage. He got out and walked around to help her out, then led her to the door into the house. Jeff stopped and knocked three times in quick succession, waited two seconds, then knocked once. From the other side of the door came two taps in response. He smiled and opened the door.

They stepped into a bright blue and white kitchen where a tall, slender woman with blond hair stood to one side with her arms crossed in front of her body. Susanna guessed she was about forty-five. When she saw Jeff, she smiled, and uncrossed her arms to reveal a Beretta hand gun, which she lay on the small counter next to her. Jeff smiled, and turned to flip the dead bolt in the door.

"Hey, stranger," she said, coming forward to give him a hug. Susanna noticed he returned the hug easily, and she found herself bristling a little. The woman broke the hug and turned to look Susanna up and down. "Is this our guest?" she asked.

"Yes," he replied, grateful she didn't refer to Susanna as the target, as she had done in the past.

"Chris, this is Susanna, Susanna, meet Chris."

"Chris!" said Susanna in surprise, "but I thought…"

"I know, I'm sorry, I didn't realize you thought Chris was a man until we were in the car, and then we got interrupted." Chris looked with amusement from Jeff to Susanna.

"Well, welcome to my home, Susanna. Can I get you anything?"

"No, thank you, we just ate."

"Come in and sit down," she said, leading the way into a cozy living room with a couch and two overstuffed easy chairs. Susanna sat on the couch and Jeff sat down next to her. Chris sat in a chair opposite them and assessed Susanna.

"Bodie said Susanna needed a safe place for a day or two. Care to fill me in on the details?" Chris looked at Jeff. Briefly, he recounted the events of the day, ending with the reason Susanna could not stay at her home tonight.

"You sure you weren't followed?" she asked.

"I'm sure," he grinned. "You weren't the only one who worked undercover," he said.

"You were an undercover cop?" Susanna exclaimed, looking at Chris.

"One of the best," Jeff answered for her. "I'd trust Chris

with my life any day. In fact," he looked at Chris, "I did, and she is the reason I am here today." Susanna sensed an invisible bond between them. Suddenly, she felt very tired and caught herself yawning.

"Let me show you your room," Chris said to Susanna. She stood and led the way to the staircase off the living room. "My room is down the little hallway, she said, motioning to the right of the stairs," in case you need anything."

Jeff followed with Susanna's bag. Chris stopped at the second room in the upstairs hallway and motioned Susanna in. The room was beautiful. It had a big double bed with a carved pine headboard and a handmade quilt for the bedspread. There were tables on either side of the bed, with matching handmade lamps fashioned from forest wood. A wooden chair was in one corner of the room, and a dresser stood against the wall, across from the bed.

"You have your own bathroom through that door," Chris pointed. "Feel free to soak in a bath or take a shower. There are towels on the racks, and an extra robe and slippers on the shelf." She glanced at Susanna's small bag, which Jeff had placed on the chair. "You will also find extra toiletries in the medicine chest if you need anything. There are bottles of water in there too, if you want one by the bed."

"A bath would be heavenly!" Susanna said, "You are so kind." Chris glanced at Jeff, then back at Susanna.

"There are a few ground rules, Susanna," she said softly. "You are on the second floor and there are no balconies. But, please do not open any windows tonight and under no circumstances are you to go outside or in the garage." She watched Susanna's face fall. She moved forward and placed her hand on Susanna's arm. "You'll wake the neighborhood when the alarms go off," she smiled. Susanna knew she was trying to make her feel better. She also knew there were no neighbors.

"If you need anything, remember I am in the room at the foot of the stairs." she studied Susanna's face. "Just call out my name, and I'll come running!" She smiled at Susanna, but she knew it was all an act to create a sense of safety. She looked at Jeff.

"Are you staying too?" she asked in a voice that quivered. Chris crossed her arms and looked at Jeff, eyebrows arched and a smirk on her face.

"Uh, about that..." Jeff started, looking at Chris. She didn't help him, she just stood and stared at him, smiling.

"You said you'd stay." Susanna looked crestfallen and uncertain.

"There is another room at the top of the stairs, if you want it, cowboy." She was grinning now. Jeff flushed and shot Chris a look that said he wished she would be quiet.

"Of course I'll stay, Susanna, I just hadn't asked Chris yet when I promised you," he said.

"Thank you. Thank you both, I don't..." her voice cracked and she stopped, bringing her hand to her mouth.

"My pleasure," said Chris, jumping in. "Why don't you go take a bath and get some rest. We'll both be here if you need anything. Try to relax." She turned and walked out of the room. Jeff looked at Susanna.

"You are safe here. I hope you can get some sleep, and remember, I am right next door if you need anything at all." Those eyes were going to rip his heart out if he stayed another second. He walked to the door and started to pull it closed. He turned back and she was still standing there. "Good night, Susanna," he said gently, and pulled the door shut behind him.

He stood outside the door for a few moments. This morning, he had not even met this woman, but tonight, she held a power over him he did not yet understand. He blew a slow breath out and shook his head, rubbing his eyes. It was sure easier to deal with her when she was arguing with him! He looked at the stairs. Susanna was settled, now all he had to do was to go downstairs and face Chris.

# Chapter 5

Susanna woke up with a start in the darkened house. She was crying, and for a few minutes, did not remember where she was. She sat up in bed and looked around, then reached to turn on the light by the bed. The light was somewhat soothing in the unfamiliar surroundings.

There was a soft tap at the door, then it opened and Jeff stood there, bare foot, bare chest, and apparently wearing only his blue jeans.
He scanned the room, lingering an extra few seconds on the window, then he walked over and tested it to make sure it was still closed and locked. He slipped the gun in his hand quickly in the back waist band of the jeans.

"I heard you cry out," he said, coming towards her. "Is everything all right?" His brow was gathered together in concern. He studied her face and noted the tears on her cheeks. Jeff reached for a tissue from the box on the night stand and sat on the edge of the bed, gently blotting the tears off her cheeks. She sat quietly, watching his face as he tenderly soaked up the tears in the tissue. She was shaking and couldn't make herself stop.

"I'm sorry I woke you. I don't know what's wrong with me," she said clasping her arms around her drawn up knees to try to stop the shivering. It wasn't cold. Her eyes caught on his well muscled, bare chest with a slight gathering of hair between his shoulders and a narrowing line down his chest to below the waist of his jeans. He wasn't wearing a shirt and he wasn't shivering.

He stopped blotting the tears away and placed two fingers on the bottom of her chin to draw her eyes back up to look at him. His eyes were deep and expressive, and the look of caring almost sent her back to tears. His hands moved to her upper arms and he gently rubbed his thumbs back and forth in what he hoped was a soothing motion.

"Susanna," he said in a deep whisper, "I will tell you again. In one day, you have been shot at, knocked to the ground by a stranger, lost your backpack with your work and identification, and had the security of your home violated." He brushed a few strands of hair back from her face. "You lost things that were important to you, family memories that you may never get back." He looked into her eyes again. "That is a lot for any person to take in one day."

If only he hadn't brought up the arrowheads. She put her head down on her knees and started to cry softly again. She felt him shift on the bed, and his arms were around her, pulling her head against his chest.

"Shhh," he said. "I'm sorry I mentioned the arrowheads," he whispered. "I will do my best to get them back for you." He was stroking her back, running his hands up and down between her shoulder blades and her waist, letting her cry.

Gradually, he became aware of the thin fabric of her nightgown and realized he had not grabbed a shirt when he heard her cry out. She had stopped shivering, but the warmth of her against his bare skin was making him uncomfortable. She had also stopped crying, and he turned his head, bending to look down at her face. She was asleep!

He watched the rhythmic rise and fall of her chest for a few minutes, taking in the wet eyelashes and the damp, soft cheeks. Her full, rosy lips were slightly parted, and he could feel the soft breath on his bare chest.

"What do I do now?" he asked himself quietly. He couldn't stay like this all night, but he hated to leave her until he was sure she would be able to rest. He held her for several more minutes, then shifted and laid her gently on the pillow. He pulled the cover up to her shoulders and reached over to the light. He remembered it had a feature to dim the light, and he did, so it left a soft night light for her in case she awakened again. Maybe she would not be so frightened if she could readily understand her whereabouts.

He stood looking at her for a few more minutes, but her breathing did not change. He turned and quietly left the room, closing the door behind him.

In the hall, he stopped and listened to the sounds in the house for several minutes. Nothing seemed out of the ordinary, so he returned to his own bed.

Jeff lay back down on the bed, loosening the button at the waistband of his jeans, but leaving them on. He was glad he chose to leave them on before, or he might have ended up in Susanna's bedroom in a very embarrassing lack of clothing.

He was tired, but his thoughts were of Susanna as he drifted back to sleep. Thoughts of how she felt through her thin night gown, nestled against his bare chest. Thoughts of how much he wanted to kiss her soft, warm lips as they rested against him. Thoughts he knew he should not be having about a witness.

Chapter 6

Susanna opened her eyes slowly. She stared at the lamp, still lit with a low glow. It was similar to the handmade lamp that had been damaged when her home was ransacked.

Slowly, she sat up, swung her legs over the side of the bed, and looked around the room. It was homey with its handmade furnishings, but it wasn't her home. She reached over and tapped the light until it turned off. There was a small plaque on the back of the lamp and she stood to get a better look. Tahoe Timber Uniques. That sounded like it was handmade, hopefully by a local crafts person. Maybe whoever made the lamp could fix the one that was so important to her. She sighed, and walked into the bathroom to brush her teeth.

Twenty minutes later, showered and dressed in her other clean tee shirt, she came down the stairs. She heard low voices in the kitchen and started in that direction, but suddenly stopped when she got close enough to understand the conversation.

"I heard you go into Susanna's room last night," said Chris. "You know I am a very light sleeper."

"I heard her cry out and went to check on her," said Jeff.

"Did you take time to put on some clothes, because I know how you sleep!" she laughed.

"Hey," laughed Jeff, "why would you remember that?"

"It was pretty unforgettable," Chris chuckled. "But seriously, did you scare her to death?"

"No!" he replied, "I slept with my jeans on last night."

"Uh huh!" she teased.

"Besides, she might appreciate my body! After all, at least one woman did once upon a time!" They both laughed.

Susanna felt the heat in her face. Were they laughing at her? Did they think she was some kind of naïve child? Obviously, Chris had seen him without clothes at some time; how close had they been? What was their relationship now?

She thought back to last night when he had held her, sitting on the edge of her bed. He had felt so strong, so warm, and so…tempting. But now, he sounded arrogant, like he really thought seeing him undressed would be something she would like? What an ego this guy had! Well, she wouldn't be caught being weak or helpless again! She took a couple of deep breaths and walked into the kitchen.

"Good morning!" said Chris, as both of them swung their eyes to her face. "Were you able to sleep?"

"A little. Thank you," Susanna said to Chris, with a weak smile. She did not look at Jeff.

"Coffee?" asked Chris, getting up and moving to the counter.

"Yes, please." answered Susanna. She pointedly ignored Jeff and walked to the window, looking at the woods through the lace curtains.

"Do you take cream?" asked Chris, noticing the deliberate avoidance of Jeff. She exchanged a questioning glace with Jeff, who shrugged his shoulders and shook his head.

"Come away from the window please, Susanna," said Jeff evenly. She remained where she was for a few more seconds and Chris and Jeff exchanged another silent signal.

"It's still not safe," said Chris gently, taking her arm and leading her to the table. "Why don't you have a seat and drink your coffee. We were just talking about the plan for today."

"Really?" Susanna said, looking at her, knowing that isn't what they were talking about at all. "I want to go home." Jeff let out an exasperated sigh and Chris looked at him.

"Susanna," she said, "it might be a day or two until it is safe for you to go home."

"Nobody tried anything last night," she said, "I was afraid for no good reason." she said. "I didn't really need anyone's help," she said, scowling at Jeff. "I just had a bad dream. No big deal." He stared at her with a blank look on his face. What the hell had he done now?

"Well," said Chris, "I have some of my famous scones in the oven and was just getting ready to scramble some eggs and then we can go from there." She walked towards the stove, raising her eyebrows at Jeff over the top of Susanna's head.

"Let me give you a hand," Jeff said, standing and walking towards the counter. He gave Chris a look that said he had no idea what was going on. He reached up in the cupboard and pulled out three plates and set them on the counter. They both glanced back at Susanna, who sat with her back to them, staring into her coffee cup. "It's going to be a long day!" Jeff whispered to Chris

The scones and eggs were done shortly and Chris served them all a plate, which Jeff took to the table. She poured more coffee and set the cream on the table. Susanna was silent as she picked at her food.

"So," began Jeff, "I think we need to go to the station and look at some pictures to see if you can recognize any of the men." Susanna didn't respond. Jeff shot Chris another look. "Even if that fingerprint we got from your home matches someone in the computer, having you identify them will help," he continued. She remained stoic, sipping her coffee as if she hadn't heard him.

"The sooner they can identify them, the sooner they may be able to catch them and you can go back to your own home," offered Chris.

"Why can't I stay at my own home tonight?" she asked stubbornly. "No offense, Chris, you have a beautiful home and I really appreciate your hospitality, but I want to go home. I need to work!"

Jeff sat back in his chair and studied her. He was trying to understand how she felt, but he was worried about her too. She was his responsibility now, and his only witness. Jeff was sure artifacts were being stolen from his jurisdiction, but Susanna was the only one who had seen them in the act. He hadn't seen anything but her, right before he heard the racking of the shotgun. He couldn't identify any of the men, and he couldn't testify as to what they were actually doing. He needed her.

"If I got you a lap top, could you do any work here?" he asked.

"Well, yeah, I could coordinate some mapping and write a

short report," Susanna replied. "I could send my findings back, and do a little research," she said, caught off guard by his offer. "But," she stiffened again, "I want to go home!"

"We know you do, Susanna, "spoke Chris. "We really do understand. We have both had to be hidden in safe houses before, and it isn't the same as being home. You feel trapped." She searched Susanna's face to see if she was getting anywhere.

"We just can't protect you at your home," said Jeff softly. "We don't even know who the bad guys are yet," he continued. "I was going to take you to the station to look at some pictures and maybe work with our sketch artist." He paused and looked at Chris for help. She took the cue.

"Right now, "said Chris, "every stranger that walks towards you is a threat. You are the only one that knows who might try to hurt you. Once we have sketches or can identify someone, it will be better." She scanned Susanna's face. "Are you up to helping us with this?" Susanna sat impassively, showing no emotion.

"How about we start with taking you down to the station, and see if we can make any progress," offered Jeff. Susanna just stared at him for several minutes. Finally, she looked down at her coffee and drank another swallow. When she looked up at him, she nodded.

"I'll just go up and get my sweater," she said, rising and taking her dishes to the sink.

"I'll get those," said Chris.

"Thank you for breakfast," said Susanna, as she turned and left the room.

"My pleasure," responded Chris. They waited until they heard the door of her room open and close upstairs. "What the hell was that?" demanded Chris, turning to face Jeff.

"Your guess is as good as mine," he replied, putting his hands up. "Last night, she seemed to be scared out of her wits, was crying, and then fell asleep on my chest."

"Your bare chest?" said Chris, arching an eyebrow.

"Come on Chris, it was the middle of the night and she

cried out. Did you expect me to take time to get dressed before I knew it was a bad dream instead of the bad guys?"

"I'm just teasing you, Jeff. I know what your standards are." She rubbed her eyes. "She is frustrating!"

"I even left the night light on for her in case she woke up again – I thought it would be easier for her to know where she was," he continued. He looked at the ceiling and shook his head. "Then, this morning!"

"She wouldn't even look at you when she came in the room," said Chris.

"Yeah! All I'm trying to do is save her life, which I already did once, I might add!"

"You sure that's all you're trying to do?" Chris said softly. Jeff looked at her.

"She's a witness, Chris." He looked into her eyes. She studied him for a few minutes, then nodded her head.

"I know," she sighed. "But what are you going to do? Lock her up?"

"Believe me, that thought has crossed my mind more than once!" he said. "She can be very difficult!"

"Really?" grinned Chris. Suddenly Jeff stood up straight.

"Wait a minute, I have an idea," he said, "I'll be right back." He left her standing in the kitchen while he stepped outside and took his phone off his belt. He came in a few minutes later, smiling. He told her his idea and she smiled as well.

"Might work," she said. "Guess I better plan dinner."

"I'm ready," said Susanna from the door. They both turned to face her.

"Just a sec," said Chris, who walked over and opened a cabinet against the wall of the kitchen, then hit a button. Several monitors inside the cabinet came to life and she studied the pictures carefully, with Jeff looking over her shoulder. "No alerts, and I don't see anything," she said to him.

"Me either," Jeff said. "I already let Bodie know we would be heading in, so he is expecting us."

"Cat and mouse?" asked Chris. He nodded.

"Until we know who we are looking for, I think that is a good idea," he said. "Okay, Susanna, this is what we are going to do," said Jeff, turning to her. He explained briefly as she stood silently, and then they all walked out to the garage together.

# Chapter 7

Susanna lay on the floor in the back seat of Jeff's car, half worried and half peeved. Was all this really necessary? In the garage, Chris had gotten into her car and Jeff had gotten into the front seat of his. They backed out in quick succession and the garage door closed. Then, the two cars went back down the side streets in a caravan until they got to Pioneer Trail. Jeff turned away from town and Chris turned towards it. They both had agreed to wind through back streets and make turns that would keep anyone trying to follow them guessing.

"We're almost at the station now," said Jeff to Susanna, but he kept his head facing forward. "Just a few more minutes and you can sit up and get out of the car." She didn't answer. He pulled up to the gate and hit a button that rolled the gate open. At the same time, he hit a text button on his phone.

He pulled the car into the sally port close to the building, then got out and opened her door. He extended his hand to help her out of the cramped position, but she did not take it. She climbed out awkwardly, feeling a bit stiff from riding on the floor. As she stood, he moved in front of her, putting her between him and the car door.

"Bodie?" he queried to make sure the deputy was ready as she emerged from the car. She turned and was surprised to see the deputy at the top of the stairs, surveying the open space beyond the gate, his hand on his weapon. Jeff took her arm and hurried her into the station while Bodie continued to watch behind them. He pulled her into a room at the side of a hallway, and dropped her arm to pull a chair out for her at a table. "Sit down and stay here," he said firmly.

"What..." she started.

"Stay here," he said again, meeting her eyes for a moment as he walked out of the room. She heard the door lock as he left.

"Damn it!" she fumed. "Tall, dark, and silent type isn't cutting it for me!" she said. "Who does he think he is, anyway!" She paced the length of the short room several times before the door opened and Bodie stepped in.

"Here are a few shots for you to look at M'am. See if any of them look like the men on the mountain." He turned to leave.

"Wait a minute!" Susanna said. "When do I get out of this...lock up!" she demanded.

"The sheriff will be in shortly," he said. "Please M'am, just take a look at the shots. We are trying to protect you," he said quietly, looking at her.

"I know," she sighed. She shouldn't take out her frustration with Jeff on Bodie. She sat down at the table and pulled one of the books over to her.

"Oh, I almost forgot! Here's some sticky notes if you find one that looks familiar," said Bodie, pulling a small pad out of his pocket and putting it on the table by her. "Just put it at the top of a page if you find anyone that you think might be one of the men you saw."

"Okay," she said, opening the first book. She sat, looking at the pages after Bodie left, feeling strangely disconcerted. What a mess. She had come back home feeling excited to be working in her old stomping grounds, where she had spent much of her early life. And here she sat, two days home, and she was in a locked room, looking for pictures of men who might want to kill her. She was stuck in a nightmare, and she couldn't get out.

She put her hands over her face, and tried not to cry again. She hardly ever cried, and now, the past twenty-four hours, it seemed like she cried at everything! She was losing her grip, and she didn't like it. What she hated most was not having any control over what she could and could not do. She felt like her life was not her own.

She just wanted to get back to work and forget all about this. She wanted to forget she had ever met Jeff. She felt like she was on a roller coaster with him, wanting to lean on him and trust him one minute, then feeling like she had to throw up her defenses against him the next. Could she really trust him? Well, she didn't have much choice right now.

Jeff looked through the window of the room, before opening the door where Susanna sat. Her head was in her hands again, leaning over the open book of mug shots. He could see she was still at the beginning of the book. How could a woman be so vulnerable, so in need of protection, and so damned difficult at the same time? He sighed in exasperation and opened the door.

Susanna jumped as he opened the door, and quickly wiped a tear from her face.

"I'm sorry," Jeff said, "I didn't mean to frighten you," he said with sincerity.

"Everything seems to frighten me these days," she responded without thinking, then bit her lip. She hadn't meant to sound so needy, like a small child. She looked up to see him studying her, and to her chagrin, he really looked like he cared. She broke the eye contact and looked back down at the book.

He pulled out a chair and sat down next to her. He took a book and opened it too, more to relieve her pressure than anything. She had given him a description of sorts, so if he saw any that looked like her description, he could ask her. She turned a page and gasped. He looked at her sharply.

"I think…"she said, pointing to a picture of a young man, "that one." Jeff pulled a pad out of his pocket and made a note.

"Was this one of the workers or the leader?" he asked.

"Just one of the helpers," she replied. He nodded.

"Keep going, please," he said. Several pages later, she stopped and tapped another picture.

"This one was there too." Again, Jeff made a note, then rose and went out the door, leaving her alone again. Bodie stepped in the door and smiled at her.

"M'am, I know this is hard for you and I know you are trying to get some work done. I want you to know my brother's wife is Washoe and her grandma is an elder that has lived here her whole life." He shifted from foot to foot and looked down at the floor for a minute. "Would it help...I mean, would you like to talk to her? I mean, my sister-in-law's grandmother? We all call her grandma." He looked at her expectantly. "She knows a lot, maybe she could help you in your research. That is, if you want."

"I...well, that would be fantastic!" said Susanna. "That would be a big help!" The smile faded from her face. "Except I have no idea when I will be free to talk to her. They want to keep me locked up." She looked down at the book on the table.

"Well, that's just the thing, M'am. I can bring her down to the station and you can talk to her here. It's not her favorite place, she likes to be outside, but she said she would do it for the Sheriff if it would help."

"The Sheriff?" said Susanna. "What does he have to do with this?" she asked.

"Well, it was his idea, M'am," said Bodie. "He thought it might help you in your work while we had to keep you, um, you know, confined." Susanna stared at him.

"Did he threaten her?" asked Susanna warily. "To try to make himself look better?" she said, her mouth a grim line.

"Why, no M'am! He wouldn't do that! All he did was ask her and she said yes!" Bodie looked appalled at the very idea.

"He just asked her and she is willing to drop everything and come talk to me?"

"Yes M'am," said Bodie. "She likes Jeff," he grinned, "in fact, sometimes I think she likes him better than me!"

"Huh." Susanna looked at Bodie, who stood waiting for her answer. "Well, it would be wonderful speaking with your grandmother, Bodie. Please tell her I appreciate it so much." She thought for a moment. "I guess you know better than I when I will be free to talk to her."

"Yes M'am," he beamed. "I'll bring her as soon as you are done," he said, smiling as he left the room.

She sat looking at the book in front of her, searching for the third man. She was confused. She couldn't figure out Jeff. And she was tired of all the disruption and see saw of emotions. She sighed as she looked through the rest of the books. She found nothing else. She could only identify two of the three she saw, and there had to be another one with the shotgun. She hadn't seen him at all.

Jeff opened the door and came back in, and stood looking at her expectantly, but she shook her head in defeat.

"No one else?" he asked.

"No," she answered, "just the two."

"Okay, well two are better than none. I'll be right back." He walked out the door again and Susanna blew a breath out in frustration.

The door opened again and Jeff came back in, followed by a young man with a sketch pad and a pencil. The young man walked around to the other side of the table and sat down.

"Susanna, this is our sketch artist, Don. If you will describe the third man, he may be able to produce a decent sketch for us to use." Don smiled and nodded as Susanna shook her head.

"Ok, well let me see. I think he was around fifty or sixty, and his face had a lot of lines on it." She paused. "I used to know a guy that drank a lot and he looked older because of the lines on his face." Don nodded.

"Oval, round, or rectangular face?" Don asked.

"Oval," she replied.

"Hair?"

"Yes," she said. She realized he was waiting for more. "Uh, light brown, thinning, looked like it had a dry, straw like texture. Not long, not short." He sketched as she spoke, but his pad was turned away from her and she couldn't see what he was doing.

"Eyes?"

"Mean," she said, then caught herself. "I couldn't tell what color they were from that distance, but they were deep set, average distance apart, and he seemed to have dark circles under them. Eyebrows were kinda bushy." He nodded.

"What about his nose," asked Don.

"Long, a little wide," she said, "almost bulbous." This was harder than she thought, trying to describe what was in her mind.

"Was his face full or thin?"

"Hmm. Average, I guess, although his cheeks were a little sunken."

"Mouth?" Don asked.

"Thin lips, kinda wide mouth. I only saw his teeth when he was threatening the one man, but they seemed average."

"What about his ears?" asked Don. She thought for a minute.

"Kinda big, "she answered, "oblong in shape." Don nodded and kept sketching. He sketched for several minutes in silence, and Susanna looked at Jeff. He was watching her, and smiled.

"Ok, let's take a look here, "said Don, turning the pad so she could see.

"Oh!" Susanna gasped, involuntarily drawing back. Her eyes were big as she stared at the drawing.

"Is it close?" asked Jeff. She nodded.

"It's him!" she said in a hoarse whisper, raising her widened eyes to look at Don. "How did you do that?" she asked.

"It's what I do," said Don modestly, a slight smile playing around his lips. "Changes?"

"No," she said, shaking her head. "It's him," she repeated.

Bodie poked his head in the door. "Sheriff?" he said, beckoning, and then walked back in the hall. Jeff got up and followed Bodie outside, where the deputy turned to face him.

"Did you find out anything about those two?" asked Jeff.

"Yeah, we did," he said. "We actually found one of them already." He cleared his throat.

"Spit it out, Bodie," said Jeff.

"We found his body," said Bodie.

"Damn it." Jeff held his breath for a minute, then exhaled and looked at the wall. "Where and when?" he asked.

"Early this morning, over by Eagle Falls," said Bodie. Some back packers coming out of Desolation saw it over the edge. Recovery team brought the body in a couple of hours ago."

"Any sign of foul play?" asked Jeff.

"Well, a little early to tell for sure, but some flags went up for the team bringing him up," said Bodie. "The trail is a little rough, and he was wearing flip flops, no jacket, no pack they could find, so no water. They didn't find a flashlight and he wasn't wearing a headlamp, but they figure he went over the edge about ten o'clock last night."

"So why was he on a rough trail after dark with no supplies, and especially without a light of some kind," pondered Jeff. "Was there any identification on the body?"

"No," said Bodie, "just a couple dollars cash in his pocket. If I hadn't run the picture Susanna picked out, we might not have caught it so quick."

"So, we have pictures of three of the men, including the sketch they are doing right now. Two are in our records, but one of those is dead." He thought for a moment. "And one is a complete mystery, the one that fired the shotgun at us." Jeff shook his head and ran a hand over his face. He looked through the window at Susanna, still talking to the sketch artist. "Tell Marty as soon as we get this sketch, to put out an All Points Bulletin for both of those men. If we can catch one of them, maybe we can identify the mystery man."

"I'll take care of it, Sheriff," said Bodie. I'll have him send the APB to all the surrounding agencies, including Game Wardens and US Forest Service personnel."

"Good, we need to catch these guys." Jeff watched her through the window for a few more minutes. "This means there is no way she can go home tonight," said Jeff. He looked at Bodie and grinned. "Would you like to tell her she has to stay at least another night in the safe house?" he asked Bodie hopefully.

"Uh, that would be a negative, sir," replied Bodie, his own grin lighting up his face. "I really think that should come from someone in a high position of authority," he said, with mock seriousness.

"Uh huh," said Jeff with resignation, "you have seen how this witness puts my authority in high esteem, right?"

"You'd be the best judge of that, sir," said Bodie hiding another smirk.

"Well," said Jeff. "What say we not tell her until after she talks to Dinah? Maybe she'll be in a better mood after that little conversation."

"Whatever you think, Sheriff," said Bodie trying hard, but not succeeding, in hiding his smile.

"Who will be in a better mood for what?" said a subdued voice. They turned to see a short, smiling woman, with beautiful skin and short, curly gray hair standing in the hall. Twinkling dark eyes peered out from behind black rimmed glasses. The colorful skirt and loose top, belted with a sash, seemed to match her brilliant smile.

"Grandma Dinah!" said Bodie. "I was going to come and pick you up! How did you get here?"

"I have been driving since before you were born, Bodie," she said patiently.

"I know, but…" he noticed the box she held. "Oh, I didn't know you had things to bring in, why didn't you tell me? I would have helped," he said, reaching for the box she carried.

"I am not helpless," the elderly woman chided, "but respect is good, so maybe you will get a taco." She grinned, knowing the Indian tacos were one of Bodie's favorites.

"Indian tacos?" said Jeff and Bodie in unison, peering into the box. A delicious aroma was wafting up from the box, making their mouths water.

"You know I brought one for you, Sheriff, and one for my new friend, too," she smiled, turning to look into the room. Her face clouded as she gazed at Susanna. "She has seen much sadness, this one," she asserted. Jeff and Bodie both looked at her, continually amazed at what she just knew. She turned back at the two men.

"Well, they aren't getting any hotter standing here." They scrambled to open the door for her, and she walked into the room, bringing with her a presence that immediately had both Don and Susanna standing. Grandma Dinah set the box on the table.

"Susanna, this is Grandma Dinah, Elder of the Washoe

Tribe," he said, introducing the women.

"I am so honored to meet you," said Susanna, "and I appreciate this time more than you can imagine." Grandma Dinah took her hands and stood, looking into Susanna's eyes for several minutes. No one moved. Then Dinah smiled, and patted Susanna's hand.

"It will be alright," she said, smiling at Susanna. Then she turned her gaze at Jeff, without letting go of Susanna's hand. "It will be alright," she said simply to him, and smiled. "Ok, everyone have a seat before these get cold," she said, breaking the spell that had hung over the room.

Don excused himself, thanking her for the invitation, but apologizing that he had to be in Placerville in a couple of hours.

"I'll give the sketch to Marty to get out to the officers and surrounding agencies," said Don.

"Perfect," said Jeff, "Marty has the other picture from our files too and is waiting for you. He is the best at getting information out through our law enforcement networks." Don left the room and Jeff turned to see the rest of them waiting, expectantly, as Dinah passed out plates of Indian tacos to everyone.

"I haven't had one of these since I was a little girl!" said Susanna. "I love Indian tacos!" she said taking a bite.

"I know," said Dinah and took a bite herself. No one asked how she knew, but they believed her.

## Chapter 8

Jeff and Bodie had their heads together with Stan and Marty as they shared ideas and strategies for trying to find the men that were a threat to Susanna, and whom they had reason to believe were stealing Washoe artifacts. They had put the pictures out to all surrounding law enforcement, but not yet to the media. They wanted these men; they didn't want them to run.

They had left Susanna and Dinah in the room, talking after lunch, having given Susanna a tablet and pen. Jeff had promised a lap top for later, but he knew Dinah would not appreciate someone talking to her with their head half buried in a computer screen. He planned to give them all the time they wanted, and he was using the time wisely while Susanna was occupied.

"Have you told her yet that she will have to stay in the safe house again tonight?" asked Bodie. Jeff shot him a look that made him squirm.

"No," he said, "and I'm not looking forward to it." He looked at the three deputies. "I sure hope we get these guys soon, or it will be hard on all of us, for many reasons." He laid another map on the big table and started to point to an area when the back door alarm went off.

"Susanna!" said Jeff as three of them raced for the back door. They ran down the hall, past the empty conference room, to the door that stood ajar at the back of the station. Jeff glanced at the monitor, but could see nothing outside the door. He unclipped his gun and drew the weapon as he carefully pushed the door open, the other deputies lined up behind him. He peered around the edge of the door and swore, putting his gun back in his holster. Bodie and Stan exchanged a look, and then Jeff pushed the door opened and stepped out on the small landing.

"Damn it, Susanna!" he snapped as she stood in the parking lot, waving goodbye to Dinah. He flashed a smile he didn't feel at Dinah and offered a wave as she drove away. He strode towards Susanna and took her arm, pulling her back in the station. "What in the hell do you think you are doing?" he demanded, letting go of her arm. Bodie and Stan faded back down the hall.

"I was helping Dinah carry the box of dishes to her car," she spat, "I didn't see anyone else offering and I thought it was the least I could do!"

"You need to get it through your head that you are in danger!" He was fuming.

"Oh good grief, are you still harping on that? We were perfectly safe!"

"If you were safe at all, it is because you are here!"

"Dinah was so nice to me, I thought the polite thing to do was to walk her to her car!"

"And what if someone had shot at you and missed...and hit her," he said quietly. Her face turned ashen as she stared at him, not breathing for a few minutes. Without a word, she lowered her eyes and walked past him to the conference room. He stood, one hand up on the wall, for several minutes. Then he shook his head. How can she make me feel like such a jerk for just doing my job? He turned and saw her sitting with her back to the door in the conference room, her things gathered in front of her.

She was just sitting there, her chin resting on her hands, staring at the wall. She didn't move, she didn't make a sound. As he watched her, he thought he preferred it when she was arguing with him. He didn't know what to do with a woman who was simply hurting. And he hadn't even told her they had to go back to Chris' tonight.

Bodie came down the hall towards him, stopping beside him and watching Susanna for a minute. Then he looked at Jeff.

"Need anything, boss?" he asked, studying Jeff's face. "You look tired."

"Yeah," Jeff answered, "I guess I am. Maybe Chris can keep watch tonight for awhile. He looked at Susanna again, then back to Bodie. "Keep an eye on her, will you Bodie? I'm going to go find a lap top she can use tonight. Don't let her out of your sight," he warned. Bodie nodded and Jeff walked down to the main room. He returned about twenty minutes later with a laptop and charger cord in his hand. Susanna was still sitting like a statue. Jeff looked at Bodie with a question on his face.

"She hasn't moved a muscle that I can see," he shrugged. "Find something?" he asked, looking at the lap top.

"Yeah, we had one in surplus. Jim wiped it and double checked it just in case, so I signed it out for her to use," he explained.

"Well," said Bodie, "I hope it helps. Anything else I can do before I go home?"

"Yeah, can you double check with Chris, make sure she is home and ready for us?"

"10-4," the deputy said, "be right back. A few minutes later, he came back and nodded. "She's all set, says you can come anytime. She will be watching for you. No activity in the neighborhood today, either."

"Thanks, Bodie," said Jeff. "Let me know if you hear anything else on those APB's tonight."

"Will do." He looked at Susanna and then back to Jeff. "You want me to keep watch while you get her in the car?"

"Thanks – probably a good idea now that we have a correlation to them and a death." He blew out a breath. "Well," he smiled wryly, guess I better go tell her." He walked into the conference room and stood for a minute behind her. She gave no indication she knew he was there. "Susanna," he said, but she did not turn to face him, so he moved around the table to face her. "Susanna," he said, "I'm sorry, but we need to go back to the safe house tonight." She didn't move. "I found you a lap top you can use until you can get your own things back." She nodded this time, and stood, gathering her things to her chest, then walked out to the hall, and stopped a few feet in front of the door. He rose and followed her, sharing a "what the hell" look with Bodie.

"Ready?" he asked the deputy. Bodie nodded and drew his weapon. Jeff took the keys out of a pocket, and unclipped his gun, putting one hand on the grip. He looked up at the monitor to the parking lot, studied it for a few minutes, then walked through the door, motioning for Susanna to follow.

He hit the key fob, unlocking the car closest to the sally port landing, and Susanna walked quickly to the door, opened it, and sat inside. Jeff got in the driver's side and started the car. He shot a look at her. She had buckled her seatbelt and was staring straight ahead.

He deftly backed the car out, pressed the button for the gate, and proceeded with evasive maneuvers, coming in the back way to the safe house. The garage door opened for the car as they drove in the driveway, and Jeff could just see Chris standing at the back of the garage, in the shadows, near the door to the house, weapon in her hand. The garage door closed behind them and Jeff got out of the car.

"Bodie told me about Eagle Falls," said Chris, by way of explaining the drawn weapon. Jeff turned to the passenger side, but Susanna was already out and walking to the door to the house. Chris opened the door and they all moved inside. Chris shot Jeff a questioning look, then smiled at Susanna. "Are you hungry?" she asked. "I made a roast with potatoes and an awesome salad."

"Thank you, I appreciate your kindness," said Susanna, smiling briefly at Chris. "I am sorry, and I hope you don't think I'm rude, but I just want to go to bed."

"Sure," Chris nodded, "whatever you would like to do is fine." Susanna turned and started towards the stairs.

"Susanna," said Jeff, "I need to bring you up to date on a few things." He had to tell her about the body they just found over the cliff near Eagle Falls. She still did not believe she was in real danger. She stopped, one foot on the bottom stair and a hand on the railing.

"Can't it wait until tomorrow?" she asked, looking up the stairs and not at him. "I'm really tired and just want to go to bed."

"Sure," he said, realizing if he told her about the body tonight she would probably have a tougher time sleeping. "Try to get some rest, and remember we are here if you need anything."

"Uh huh," she mumbled, as she walked up the stairs.

# Chapter 9

"That was a great dinner, thank you, Chris," said Jeff as they sat in the living room with coffee. The dinner was done, table cleared, and dishes in the dishwasher. He sipped his coffee, freshly made from home ground beans and smiled. He really enjoyed a good cup of coffee.

"Thank you!" Chris smiled, as she sat and pulled her legs up under her in the big overstuffed chair next to her fireplace. "I don't cook much anymore; it's good to know I still have the touch!" She studied his face, lined with fatigue. "So," she said, lifting her own cup to her lips, "Bodie gave me the condensed version. Especially given the behavior of our guest, would you like to fill in the details for me?" Jeff looked at her and ran his hands through his hair.

"Chris, I've had to protect a lot of witnesses and you know this isn't my first rodeo with either witnesses or women, but this one!" He let out an exasperated sigh.

"Why don't you just start at the beginning, and I will see if anything different pops out from my perspective." She settled in deeper to the chair and focused on Jeff, listening intently to each description. He sat, staring into his coffee cup, thinking.

"Does Susanna know about the one man being found at Eagle Falls trail?" Chris prompted.

"No, I was going to bring her up to date before I brought her out here. I thought getting to talk to Dinah would be a good thing for her, so I waited until after they were done. When she went outside with Dinah, I realized I should have told her."

"So she wouldn't have gone outside," said Chris, nodding her head in understanding.

"Yes," said Jeff. "Then, I thought she would object to coming to the safe house again tonight, so I was going to tell her right before we left the station, hoping she wouldn't argue." He chewed on his lower lip, and shook his head again. "But, she didn't argue, so I thought I would wait until I got her here."

"Because she wouldn't be as difficult on the drive here,"

observed Chris. She could still read his mind, even though it had been years since they were partners.

"Yes," said Jeff again. "And just now, I was going to tell her, but realized it might make it harder for her to get any sleep tonight, so I didn't tell her." He looked at his old partner. "I feel like I am hanging onto a moving pendulum with this one, Chris. I've never had a witness fight so much against protection. She just won't believe she is in any danger!"

"She is a feisty one, that is for sure," said Chris, thinking.

"I can't believe the way she argues with me over everything!" He took another sip of coffee.

"Really?" Chris grinned. "Big, strong, good looking lawman has met a woman that does not fall at his feet in adoration?" she teased.

"Come on, Chris," Jeff colored, "I'm not like that," he said. He looked at her. "Am I?" he asked, his face showing doubt.

"No, Jeff, you aren't like that. "You are level headed and logical, and I have never known you to be conceited about your rugged good looks."She smiled at him as a blush rose in his cheeks. "But this is a tough one. With little hope we will find them quickly, and with one we can't even identify, she is not going to be happy." She looked at Jeff. "She came home to work on something about which she is very passionate, and she stumbled on something that made her a prisoner in my home," she said softly. "She can't even go outside."

"I know, and I feel bad for her, but I would never forgive myself if I slipped up and she ended up dead." He looked back at Chris. "She is the only witness, and that makes this all the more dangerous."

"I get that," said Chris, "we've done this a time or two, even together. And we have both learned a thing or two." Suddenly, she broke into a huge grin. "Like to sleep with some clothes on when we are on protection detail," she laughed.

"Hey, that was my first detail, and I wasn't thinking," he said, shifting in his seat. "I went to bed like I always do."

"And when the shooting started, you came running,

without a stitch on!" she giggled. "I nearly dropped my weapon when I saw yours just hanging out there!" she was holding her side now, almost rolling with laughter.

"I just came with my gun as soon as I heard the first shot!" said Jeff defensively.

"Oh, you certainly did!" she chuckled. "I thought the guy we were shooting at and his girlfriend would drop their guns as soon as they saw you, streaking buck naked through the door into the room they had breached!"

"Well, we got them, didn't we?" Jeff asked, hoping to end this part of the conversation.

"Oh yeah, we sure did! And the girlfriend couldn't stop staring at your ah, attributes, while you held the gun on her. And you, without a Stetson to help you out!" She was choking on her laughter now.

"Having fun?" said Jeff, scrunching up his mouth in an expression that said enough is enough.

"And then when you tried to cover your um, parts, with one hand while still keeping the gun on them, the girl laughed and she said…" Chris could not speak as the laughter bubbled out of her. "… and she said to you, 'one hand ain't nearly big enough, cowboy' and laughed at you! I thought you were going to die of embarrassment!" She had to put her coffee on the table beside her and leaned forward with her hands on her stomach, still laughing.

"I don't remember it being that funny," he said, straight faced.

"Oh, oh, and then when you asked that other officer if you could borrow his Stetson for a few minutes, and he looked at you and said, oh my God, this hurts," she said, holding her stomach. "He looked at you and said," she continued, "… 'you ain't putting that thing in my hat' and you looked like you wanted to shoot him!" She was laughing so hard tears were coming out of her eyes.

Jeff stood. "More coffee?" he offered.

"Yes, please," she said, trying to bring her laughter under

control as he walked to the kitchen with their cups. By the time he returned, she was calm, but still smiling.

Jeff handed her the cup of coffee, and then frowned. He sat down opposite her and then looked at her with concern.

"Susanna doesn't need to know that story," he started, but Chris held up a hand.

"My lips are sealed," said Chris, "and I'm sorry. It just popped in my head tonight and maybe I thought we could both use a little tension relief. I don't know." She looked at him and he chuckled.

"Okay, it was pretty funny looking back," he smiled at her, "but I would appreciate it if that story stays between us."

"Absolutely," she nodded, and Jeff breathed a sigh of relief. "Now, tell me exactly, step by step, what went on at the station, "said Chris. "Something has a hold of that girl, something happened to change her from the time she left this morning."

Jeff went through everything that had happened. Chris nodded a few times, but did not say much, until he told the part of the story that had Susanna walking Dinah out to her car.

"Is that when her manner changed?" asked Chris.

"After I chewed her out for being stupid enough to go outside without an escort?" said Jeff. "Yeah, I think so, but I have said things like that to her before and all she does is bicker; it doesn't affect her."

"Exactly what did you say when you got her back inside the station?"

"I asked her what the hell she thought she was doing..." Jeff thought for a minute. "Then I told her she could get shot, and she told me I was basically blowing everything out of proportion." Jeff shook his head, trying to remember every detail.

"Did you say anything else?" asked Chris. Jeff was concentrating, when suddenly he froze.

"I asked her how she would feel if someone shot at her and missed and hit Dinah." he said. "That's exactly when she turned quiet and went and sat in the conference room." He scratched his head, then stood and walked to the window, peeking through the curtains. He turned and looked at Chris. "Are you thinking the same thing I am?" he asked. Chris nodded her head.

"It was one thing when it was just her safety. She could push that away and not think about it." Chris looked at him. "Even with you, she might think nothing would happen to you because you are the sheriff and have a gun to defend yourself. But the thought of other people getting hurt because of what she knows just may have kicked her into the dark side of all this." Jeff blew out a long breath and they looked at each other for a few minutes.

"I had to make her realize the danger," said Jeff. "She thinks she is immortal!"

"I know," said Chris, holding up a hand. "You are doing your job. You have no control over how she will react." She motioned for him to sit again. "Now, my thoughts on this situation," said Chris. Jeff looked at her expectantly. She still had great instincts and he respected her insight. "You need to go catch the bad guys," she said, looking him squarely in the eye. "You are too valuable to be on protection duty."

"I agree, I only stayed because she seemed so alone and asked me to, but frankly," he paused, looking down at the floor, "she quarrels with me about everything, so maybe it is best if I just leave her here." Chris nodded.

"Have you had a chance to think about who might be receiving the stolen goods?" she asked.

"No, and you are right, I need to be focusing on solving the crime and not be distracted with protection duty."

"She can do some work here, and I will be fine protecting her. Maybe send out Stan, if you want, in plain clothes, please, so he doesn't draw attention."

"I want two of you here with her," said Jeff, "I know there are at least three bad guys out there, maybe more." Chris nodded agreement.

"Tell him to bring some groceries, I don't want to leave her with just one of us and I won't take her with me," said Chris. "It would be impossible to protect her when we don't know who we are looking for, other than the fact they are men."

"Okay," he nodded, then bit his lower lip. "She is going to need more clothes, she didn't bring much with her. I didn't think she would be here that long." He stood up and paced for a minute. "I'll take her tomorrow morning, first thing," he said, "I know she won't be happy if I pick them out for her, or even you, for that matter."

"Do you want to do cat and mouse again?" asked Chris.

"Yeah, but with a switch," he said, thinking for a minute. "We will put Susanna in your car and I'll drive and you take my car...and maybe wear my hat," he said, looking to see her reaction. Chris got up and went to the closet. She opened the door and reached in, pulling out a big jacket and a hat. She put on the jacket and then pulled her hair up and placed the hat on top of her head.

"How about you keep your Stetson on the seat and I wear my own?" she grinned. "We won't fool anyone really scrutinizing us carefully, but if we whip out of here, anyone watching may be temporarily confused, and that could be enough."

"Lady, I like your style!" he said.

"I know," she grinned back, "I am the only woman badass former cop that can keep up with you!" They both laughed.

"Good, we'll get that done first thing, then I will bring her back to you and she can stay put for a few days. I can get more work done on the case without worrying about her." Suddenly he yawned. "I am really tired," he said, rubbing his eyes.

"I can imagine! You have been hitting it pretty hard yourself the past couple of days. Why don't you hit the sheets?" she suggested. "I took a nap today in case I needed to stand watch all night. Now that you have likely tied them to a murder, we need to be more careful." She studied his face. "Frankly, you look like you are ready to sleep on your feet. Go to bed, I got this," she offered.

"You sure?" he asked, afraid to be too hopeful.

"Yes, I am sure. Stan and I will take turns sleeping tomorrow too, so neither of us will get too tired." She smiled at him. "Good night, cowboy."

"Night M'am," he said, grinning at her. He walked up the stairs and paused at Susanna's door, listening. He heard nothing, so he took a chance and quietly opened the door to look in.

She was sleeping, with the night light feature giving a soft glow to her face. He shut the door carefully and turned to his own room. She looks so sweet when she is sleeping, he thought.

As he lay down on the bed, he felt the tension in his shoulders start to slip away. He wanted to take off his jeans and really get comfortable, but the reminder Chris had given him overpowered that thought. Instead, he settled for no shirt, no boots, no socks, and a couple of buttons undone on his jeans. He was asleep in minutes.

# Chapter 10

Chris tapped lightly on Susanna's door the next morning about eight o'clock. Breakfast was ready, but it was to check on her as well, since neither of them had actually put eyes on her since last night.

"I'm ready," said Susanna, opening the door. Chris noted she was in the same clothes as yesterday. She did need a change or two, so they could at least put a few things in the washer between wearing them, thought Chris. This could go on for another week.

Chris led the way downstairs to where Jeff was pouring coffee into three mugs, which he then set on the table. He looked up as they walked into the dining area.

"Did you get any sleep, Susanna?" he asked, studying her face. It seemed to him there were dark circles under her eyes. She hadn't cried out last night, but he still woke a few times just to listen.

"Some," she said, still avoiding his eyes. They all sat down at the table, and served themselves some muffins and fresh fruit with their coffee. Jeff looked at Chris, then at Susanna, who was picking at her blueberry muffin.

"Susanna, I am going to take you to your house today to pick up a few more changes of clothing," he said. Her face lifted and for a brief instant, a smile almost lit her face. Then it was gone.

"That must mean I am going to have to stay here a few more days," she said dejectedly.

"Yes," said Jeff. "I didn't have time to tell you yesterday, Susanna, but we found one of the men you identified in the book."

"That's good then, maybe he can tell you where the others are!" she exclaimed hopefully.

"No," Jeff shook his head, "he can't tell us anything, Susanna." He paused, and shot Chris a glance. "He's dead."

She jerked as if he had struck her and jumped up so fast,

her chair nearly fell over. She walked rapidly back and forth, her hands first on her head, then her arms crossed in front of her.

"I don't like this," she said, "this has to stop now! Why don't you stop this?" she yelled at Jeff, a wild look in her eye. "You need to catch them so they can't hurt anyone else and so I can have my life back!" Her hands were on her hips now and she was leaning towards him.

"Susanna," Chris interjected, "that is what we are all trying to do. Jeff will take you to get some more clothes and a few other things you may want or need, and then he will bring you back here so he can concentrate on finding the thieves," said Chris firmly, hoping the no nonsense tone in her voice would calm Susanna. "I do have a washer and dryer, so once we get you a few sets of clothes, we will be able to keep some fresh all the time," offered Chris.

"I'm sorry, Susanna," said Jeff, but you will have to work here. We will do our best to get you what you need for the research and writing you need to do, but the field work is just going to have to wait."

"But I need to be on that mountain doing my work!" Her face was flushed. "You don't understand!"

Jeff looked down at the table, then slapped his hands down on the surface, and rose slowly, his eyes narrowed as they seemed to glitter with anger.

"What I understand is there are men out there trying to kill you." Jeff said as he stood, his own face growing red with aggravation. "What you need to understand is that you will not go near that mountain until we catch the men trying to kill you!" He scowled at her, as if daring her to challenge him. "If you go anywhere near that mountain until we arrest those men, you will endanger not only your life, but that of my officers!" He stood, glaring at her. "I will not tolerate any of that, do you understand?" He was almost shouting at her.

"I have to work!"she screeched, showing her agitation.

"And I have to keep you and my officers alive!" he snapped back. "There will be no more discussion on this; we do this my way, and you will do as I say in this!"

No one was interested in finishing breakfast, so Chris cleared the dishes while Jeff and Susanna glowered at each other in stony silence. They finished breakfast and got Chris dressed like a cowboy, then went into the garage and dispersed into the vehicles in the manner Chris and Jeff had discussed the night before. They exited the neighborhood without incident, and no one seemed to be watching the safe house.

---

It wasn't long before Jeff pulled up on the dirt road behind Susanna's home. He cut through the forest on the way over, explaining to her that it would be safer to come in from the back. Most of the neighborhoods in Tahoe were open; people did not always fence their yards, and this was true with Susanna's home. They walked up to her back door and Jeff took out a key he had gotten from the locksmith.

"Nice. You have a key to my home and I don't," she said, still sulking. Jeff started to speak, but she just put up a hand and shook her head. She walked through the door ahead of him, and stopped a few feet in. Someone had made an effort to restore some order, at least in the living room and dining room area. She moved into the living room, and turned around, surveying the room. She leaned over and adjusted a curtain on the window looking out into the front of the house.

"Once we got all the evidence and photographs we needed, I asked a couple of the deputies to at least straighten it a little for you," said Jeff from over her shoulder.

"Thank you," she said, giving him a look of surprise. She started down the hallway to her bedroom. They had done the same there, righted the furniture and even remade the bed with clean sheets. Her clothes had been hastily thrown in drawers, but they seemed to have been somewhat organized.

She opened the closet door and took out the spare back pack she kept on the closet shelf. Susanna opened the different drawers, and took out articles of clothing, refolding some to her liking. She stacked a few on top of the dresser, then looked around the room. She put her hand on the stack of clothes and stood for a minute, not moving them to the pack. She looked at the stack of clothes, then turned to Jeff.

"Is there any way I could take a quick shower and change into some clean clothes?" She watched his face register surprise, then observed a struggle going on in his head. "I have been in these same clothes for two days now. Three for my jeans." She looked at him, imploring him with her eyes.

"I think it would be best to wait until you got back to the safe house," he said, and saw her face cloud over.

"Please," she said. "I promise I won't be more than ten minutes, tops. I won't put on any make up and I won't do anything but wash my hair quickly. It won't take long." She stared into his eyes. "I just want to feel clean again," she said.

He walked over and checked the windows again to test the locks. Then he turned and looked at her. It was against his better judgment, but Dinah was right. She had been through a lot.

"Okay," he said, "but ten minutes tops, and I am timing you starting now." She started towards the bathroom, then turned to him.

"Are you going to wait right there?" she asked, seeming a little embarrassed. He looked at the stack of clothes on the dresser, and realized she might come out of the bathroom in a towel and want to dress in her room.

"I'll wait in the living room," he said. He pulled the door to her bedroom shut as he heard the bathroom door close and the shower start. He walked down the hall to the living room. Jeff surveyed the neighborhood through the front windows, seeing nothing unusual.

He noted Bodie had returned her car to the driveway and smiled. He sat down on the couch and put his head back, listening. Then, he got up and walked through the front area, testing doors and windows again. He checked his watch. It had been ten minutes and the shower was still running. He frowned.

If she was still in the shower, this was going to take more than ten extra minutes.

"I should have known better," he said aloud as he walked to the kitchen window and looked out at his car on the dirt road behind the house. He looked at his watch again. Fifteen minutes. He sighed and started down the hall.

"Susanna?" he called as he approached the bedroom. No answer. "Susanna?" he called again as he walked in the bedroom. Something wasn't right; she should be answering him. Suddenly he noticed the clothing on the dresser was gone, as was the backpack. In two strides he was at the bathroom door, where he pounded loudly. "Susanna! Open this door right now or I'm coming in!"

There was no answer, and he tried the door. Locked. He had no choice. Damn it! He stepped back and kicked the door in and was met with banks of rolling steam coming out of the bathroom. He walked in, waving the steam away, and then he saw it.

The bathroom window was open and she was gone! He heard an engine start and raced for the front of the house. Through the window, he saw her car backing out of the driveway! Jeff ripped open the front door and ran out in the yard.

He could see Susanna in the driver's seat, but did not see anyone else in the car with her. She looked at him for a few seconds, shook her head, put the car into gear and drove off down the street, as he ran towards the car.

"Susanna! Get back here!" he roared, knowing it was futile. He ran around the side of the house and sprinted for his own vehicle, yelling an all points bulletin on her car into the phone as he ran. He jumped into the car, swearing vehemently and profanely as he whipped the car around and started in the direction he had seen her drive.

"Damn that woman!" he yelled to no one, slamming the heel of his hand down on the steering wheel. "She's determined to get herself killed!" He sped through the neighborhood as fast as he dared, looking down every street as he drove. He was

LEAVING THE SHOWER RUNNING.

fuming. "Safe house, my ass! When I catch her this time, she's going in a jail cell!"

If I can find her before they do, he said to himself. He drove every back street he could think of for over an hour before he gave up. He swung back by her house and secured the front door, then went back to the station.

---

He walked in and was met with silence. There was lots of activity, but mostly it seemed designed to stay away from him. No one met his eyes or looked up to acknowledge his presence. He put his Stetson down on the desk and sat on the corner, surveying his officers. He ran a hand over his face, pinched the bridge of his nose, and then stood up.

"Okay, everyone, come on over here please," he said loudly. The officers looked at each other, put down files they were holding, and came slowly over to gather around his desk.

"I made a rookie mistake," he confessed to the men and women around the desk. They were embarrassed for him, and looked at their shoes or the ceiling at first. "I trusted my witness too much; I thought she understood the gravity of the situation and the danger to herself." He stopped, looking into the faces of his officers. "Against my better judgment, I let her take a shower and change her clothes." Someone snickered and he felt his face burn a little. "I know, like I said, stupid mistake. I thought we had her trust."

He shifted his weight, then met their eyes, his face now set in a grim expression. "This witness is now to be considered hostile. Her life is in danger, and she is the only witness to felonies and possibly, the only witness that could identify a murder suspect. She is not armed, as far as we know, but the men after her are, so proceed with caution." He scanned the group again, making eye contact, seeking purchase.

"Apprehend her if you can, and put cuffs on her until we

get her to a cell. We are done playing nice," he snapped. "Circulate her picture around town and see if anyone has seen her. You should all have pictures of the men we are looking for as well, at least two of them." He looked at the serious faces around him. "I don't have to tell you," he said, "be careful out there. Report in with anything you see or find, no matter how small. Let's go!"

The officers dispersed to their vehicles and hit the streets, looking for the woman and the two men. Jeff stood, watching them go, and wondering where the hell she had gone.

# Chapter 11

Susanna looked at Jeff as she shifted the gear into drive. He was so angry, his face was red as he ran towards her, yelling for her to stop. It was a dirty trick, and a part of her felt bad for him. She knew he would take a real beating emotionally and professionally for losing his witness.

She stepped on the gas and sped up the road, away from him, as fast as possible. The words he said to her yesterday kept echoing through her head: "What if someone shot at you and missed and hit Dinah?" She couldn't handle that; innocent people getting hurt because of her.

And just what did he mean about them missing her? Would he be okay if she got shot, but not Dinah? She could not figure him out. One minute he was doing something sweet, like getting Dinah there to help her work while she was in protective custody. The next minute, he was concerned about finding the men who were stealing the artifacts and trying to shoot her. Then he seemed angry with her, when she just wanted to be able to do her job.

It was too much for her right now. She had to get away. If anyone was going to be hurt, then let it be her. And, she had to work. She could stay away from where the men had been seen; she could go on the other side of the mountain and probably find things that would authenticate the hypothesis she was trying to prove.

She thought about where she could go. She had left on a sudden impulse, without giving much thought to what she would do once she got away. She always kept a sleeping bag in the trunk of her car, and now she had a pair of work boots, a few pairs of jeans, some tops, changes of underwear and socks, and a jacket. She didn't dare go to a motel, and she didn't have much money anyway. Well, camping out seemed to be her best option, and she was good at it.

She had to get to her bank. She had called her bank when she lost her card in her back pack, but she could go in and get a new card and some cash. Then she would stop at Scotty's and grab a few other things, and run into a grocery store for some food and water supplies.

She didn't think they would expect her to do what she was doing, at least she hoped not. She planned to get out of town before they really ramped up the search for her. If they did. Maybe all Jeff really wanted was to catch the thieves in the act. It wouldn't matter then, what happened to her; he wouldn't need her as a witness. Maybe all of them would leave her alone and she could get back to doing the work she loved, outside, in the fresh air.

---

Gary smiled into the phone as he waited for the other end to pick up.

"What?" came the curt greeting, which was what Gary expected.

"She just left her house, Boss," he said. "Your hunch was good, she came back. She came around the side of the house a few minutes ago and got in her car, just like you thought she might."

"You better be following her!" snapped the Boss. He never seemed to be in a good mood.

"I put a tracking device on her car last night, after dark when none of the neighbors would see me, "he said. "I know exactly where she is."

"Where's the bumbling sheriff and his band of dumb deputies?"

"He came running out of the house, madder than a wet cat, yelling at her to stop." Gary chuckled. "Must have given him the slip and made him look like a clown!" Gary surveyed the neighborhood, making sure no other officers arrived on the scene. "I think he was parked on the dirt road behind her house, 'cause he sure took off running fast and then a dark SUV ran the stop sign at the corner, taking off like a bat outta hell in her direction."

"Did he see you?" demanded the boss.

"No, I'm sure he didn't even notice me sitting over here.

Besides, I'm not the one she got a look at, am I?" he taunted. He knew the boss would be livid, but he also knew how far he could push. Gary was not a young kid, like the two the boss had killed.

One had just stumbled on the project, like the girl, but she got away because of that damn sheriff! The other two weren't so lucky. Gary shivered just thinking about it.

The first was a lone hiker who was at the wrong place at the wrong time. He had just walked up to them, a Pacific Crest Trail hiker looking for some social talk and he thought they had a camp. He smiled at them and the boss just pulled a gun out of his waistband and shot him, without a word, in cold blood.

It was the damnest thing Gary ever saw. All the kid did was come on the camp and smile, and then he was gone. The boss had him and Gordy throw him in the back of one of the trucks and drive him a couple miles away, then throw him down some ravine. Trouble was, the kid's pack caught on some tree root on the way down and ended up hanging halfway between the top and bottom of the ravine. Some other hikers saw him and reported it. The Boss was really spitting nails over that one; he didn't think they would find the body until after they were out of the area.

Then there was Gordy. Gary hadn't been sure the kid had the stomach for all this from the beginning. Stealing was one thing, but he didn't like the hiker getting shot. He wasn't comfortable with looking for the girl and being told she had to be killed either. Gary knew he was next the day he caught the Boss staring at Gordy as he worked. Gary shuddered. The Boss was an evil man, who would do or say anything to get what he wanted. Gordy showing weakness was not what the Boss wanted.

That same night, the Boss had called Gary and Gordy and told them to meet him half way up the Eagle Falls trail at ten o'clock at night. He told Gordy he couldn't get hold of Juan, so he needed Gordy and Gary to help him with the girl.

He told Gordy that the girl had been seen camping up there and they needed to see if they could find her. It would be better to take care of her in the dark; it would be harder to be seen by any witnesses.

Gordy had complained, saying he was at a bar in Homewood in flip flops, but the Boss told him to get out front and he would pick him up. Gordy didn't stop to wonder how the Boss knew the girl was in the area.

Gary and the Boss had headlamps and they lit the trail with Gordy in between them. At a steep drop off overlooking a stream, the Boss had hit Gordy in the head with a rock, insuring he wouldn't know to scream. When he stumbled, the Boss had pushed him over the side, throwing the rock after him. They could hear his body hitting the rocks on the way down. Even if the fall didn't kill him, the exposure and blood loss would.

Gary had made the Boss go first back down the trail, which caused the Boss to be furious, but he also knew Gary was armed and had a lot more experience than Gordy.

---

Susanna went to her bank first, cautiously parking on the side towards the back, where she hoped her car would be less likely to be seen. She looked around as she got out, and did not see any suspicious cars or law enforcement vehicles.

She walked quickly, and as she entered the bank, breathed a sigh of relief. There was no line, and one of her favorite tellers waved a cheerful greeting to her as she walked in.

"Hi Chrissy," she smiled, "I lost my debit card and need to get a replacement," said Susanna.

"I would be happy to do that for you," said Chrissy. It only took Susanna a few minutes to get a temporary debit card and three hundred dollars in cash.

"Going on a trip?" asked the teller, as she counted out the bills to Susanna.

"Just being prepared," laughed Susanna. "Do you have any trips planned?" she asked Chrissy, diverting the focus away from herself.

"My friend and I are leaving for a week in the Grand

Canyon next week!" bubbled the teller, clearly excited. "We're going to ride the burros down the trail to the bottom, then stay for a few days by the river! They have little cabins." They chatted for a few more minutes before Susanna wished her a wonderful vacation and walked out of the bank.

Next stop, Scotty's, she said to herself, and drove the few blocks to the small hardware store. This will be harder, she thought, she just might see a clerk that had known her for awhile. But, she knew the store, so she could find what she needed quickly. It was a small store though, which meant it would be easier to see her if anyone was watching.

"Geez, aren't you getting to be paranoid!" she scolded herself, as she parked the car and went inside. She picked up a small tarp, some rope, and a headlamp. She walked up to the counter, hoping to pay quickly. No such luck.

"Susanna!" said Robert, turning from the key machine. "It's good to see you!" He handed the key to a customer, then rang up the sale. Blaze walked around the corner from the back of the store and smiled when he saw her.

"I was sure sorry to hear about your grandfather," said Blaze. "I haven't seen you to express my condolences."

"Yeah," said Robert, "he was a good man."

"Thank you," said Susanna, with a small smile. They expressed sympathy over her grandfather again, then asked how her brother was doing. She replied that she hadn't heard from her brother in awhile.

"Looks like you are going camping," said Patrick, coming down the stairs.

"Oh, just replenishing my standard supplies," she laughed. "Sorry, guys, I have to get going, but I'll be back to catch up soon!" She waved and smiled as she scooted out the door. Popping her trunk, she threw the supplies in and quickly slipped behind the wheel again.

"Whew!" she breathed as she started the car again, "small towns are nice, but hard to be in a hurry." She was worried that Jeff would have all his people out looking for her, and she was pushing the odds.

Now, where to get groceries? Go into the closest store and hope she wasn't noticed? Or go to a convenience store and risk not getting all she wanted? She pondered for a few more minutes, then decided on an in between solution. Reasoning that they couldn't watch then all at once, she avoided Raley's and the 7-11 and opted for Grocery Outlet. She could go around the back way and park on a street by the back entrance and be in and out with less chance of being seen.

She was betting on the fact Jeff would have driven around trying to find her before going back to the station to mobilize the search. That could buy her precious minutes. She thought of Jeff's face as he stood in the driveway yelling at her to come back, and she felt a chill. If the law caught her, he would be furious and there was no telling just what he would do. She didn't want to find out.

"Well, I am a full grown woman and I have a job to do, so I will take my chances," she said aloud. Trouble was, she didn't sound all that convincing, even to herself.

She walked quickly into Grocery Outlet and picked up a couple of jugs of water, even though she always had a water purification system in the trunk, as well as a mess kit, first aid box, and basic supplies, like matches. All those things often came in handy in her line of work.

She picked up some protein bars, hot cocoa mix, instant soup, a cheap metal pan, bread, and a jar of mixed peanut butter and jelly. It was probably more than she needed, but she would rather have too much than have to come back and take a chance on getting caught.

She also bought a cheap cooler to put the food in, hoping the bears would not smell it in the trunk of her car. On impulse, she also bought some heavy duty, extra large trash bags. She could slip one around the cooler for added measure. Feeling ready to camp out for several days, she looked carefully around as she left the store. Now, all she had to do was get out of town without being spotted.

---

Gary was following the blip on the tracker as Susanna wove her way up and around the mountain. It looked like she was going right back where they had first seen her! He watched a little longer to be sure, then reached for his phone.

"Stupid bitch," he grinned. "Just drive right back into the spider's web." He hit the redial button on his phone. "Hey Boss," he said into the phone, "you aren't going to believe this!"

## Chapter 12

Jeff couldn't remember the last time he was this mad. He had fallen for one of the oldest tricks in the book, and the witness he himself had decided to protect, had escaped on his watch. She had made a fool out of him, and she did it on purpose.

His officers had tried not to blame him, and several had even told him you couldn't protect someone who didn't want to be protected, she was wearisome, it could happen to any of them...but, it still stung. He was their leader and he had made a huge mistake. He was disgusted with himself.

He was also really worried. Susanna refused to accept that her life was at risk. He had done everything he could think of to convince her that she was in severe danger, that they would be looking for her, and she had ignored his warnings. She had also deliberately disobeyed his commands, and run away in spite of the fact she could get herself or one of his officers killed.

He stared at the map in front of him, stretched out on the big conference room table. Where would she go? She had clothes and a car, but did she have any money? If her identification was in the backpack she left on the mountain, along with her debit card, did she have another credit card? How would she buy gas or food?

"Of course!" he exclaimed, walking swiftly down the hall to the file cabinet where he had placed the first report. He pulled it and read the name of her bank from the information he had taken from her. He hit the keypad and dialed. When the bank answered, he asked for the manager. He identified himself and asked if Susanna Warren had come in.

"I'm sorry, sir," said the man on the other end of the phone. "We cannot give that kind of information over the phone. We would have to see your identification in person."

"Can't you see I am calling from the Sheriff's Department?" he said, failing to hide his exasperation.

"Um, no sir," said the manager, clearing his throat, "actually, I can't, the number is blocked."

Jeff clenched his teeth, remembering the fairly new policy of blocking the number for outgoing calls. "I'll be there myself in a few minutes."

"That will be fine, sir," said the manager and hung up.

Jeff strode rapidly to his car and jumped in, driving as fast as he dared out of the parking lot. He debated whether to stick the light up on top of the car, but held the impulse in check. A few minutes later, he pulled into the bank parking lot and getting out of the car, he walked briskly into the bank. He spotted the manager immediately, sitting behind a desk off to the side.

"I'm Sheriff Clellan," he said, walking up to the seated man, pulling his credentials as he approached. The bank manager eyed the identification carefully, then stood, and came quickly around his desk.

"I hope you understand…" he began, but Jeff waved him off and forced a smile.

"I understand," he said impatiently, "but I need to know if Susanna Warren has been in this bank this morning?" The banker sat back down, tapped a few keys on his computer, then nodded.

"Yes, she was in about half an hour ago and withdrew three hundred dollars in cash."

"She lost her bank card a few days ago," said Jeff, "did she get a replacement card?"

"Let's ask the teller," said the manager, walking over to a pretty young woman, who was just finishing with a customer. Her dark brown hair shone almost as much as her beautiful smile.

"Chrissy, the Sheriff needs to talk to you about a recent transaction with a customer," said the manager.

"Of course, "she said, turning towards Jeff. "What can I do for you?"

"Can we talk in private?" Jeff asked the manager, as he noticed two customers walking through the door.

"Is something wrong?" asked Chrissy, her face changing from a smile to concern.

"No M'am," said Jeff gently as he realized she was probably racking her brain to recall if she had made any mistakes.

"I just need some information, if you don't mind." The manager guided them into a small office and the three of them sat around the small table.

"Did you wait on Susanna Warren this morning?" asked Jeff, trying to keep his voice even.

"Oh, yes," she responded, smiling. "Susanna is one of my favorite customers! She is always so nice!"

Maybe to you, thought Jeff. "Did you issue her a new temporary bank card?" he asked.

"Why, yes! She reported her old one lost several days ago, so that was not unusual."

"Does she usually withdraw a large amount of cash like that?"he asked.

"No, in fact, I asked her if she was going on a trip," replied Chrissy.

"What did she say," he asked, leaning forward and listening carefully to the answer.

"Oh, let me think," said the teller. "She said…she said 'you never can tell' and then asked me if I was going to travel soon." She looked at Jeff, worry on her face.

"Were those her exact words?" he asked.

"Yes," said Chrissy. "I hope she is alright," she said, looking from her manager to Jeff. "Is she in some kind of trouble?"

"I hope not," said Jeff. "Thank you, you have been very helpful." She got up to leave and go back to her window. He turned to the manager.

"Can you see if she has used that card anywhere since she left the bank?" asked Jeff.

"Of course," said the manager, "I just need to go back to my desk." Reaching his desk, he sat down and tapped the keys swiftly. "Yes," he said, nodding his head, "she used it about twenty-five minutes ago at Scotty's Hardware, and then twenty minutes later, at Grocery Outlet."

"Thank you," said Jeff. He got up and left the room, pushing buttons on his phone as he walked out the door.

"Bodie," he said, "she has a new bank card and cash and used the card at Grocery Outlet about ten minutes ago. Put it out that she may still be in the vicinity and see if any of our people can spot her car. I'm going to head over there and see what she bought and if she said anything. Send a unit over to Scotty's to see what she bought there. Then, we'll compare notes."

"Roger that, " said Bodie, and hung up.

Jeff walked into Grocery Outlet and asked for the managers. Kim and Mike were both in the office when he walked up and showed them his credentials. Briefly, he told them the situation and what he was hoping to find.

"What can we do to help?" asked Mike. "I don't know if we can tell quickly which register she was at or who rang her up, but we will do our best."

"Have any of the cashiers gone to break or off shift in the past fifteen minutes?" Jeff asked.

"No," said Kim, looking at the register stands. "Not yet. Do you have a picture of the woman?"

"Yes," said Jeff, pulling out his phone and bringing it up. He turned the phone so they could see the picture. They looked at each other and shrugged their shoulders.

"We haven't seen her," said Kim, "but maybe one of the checkers will recognize the picture."

"Let's go see who you need to talk to then," said Mike. It only took a few minutes for one of the cashiers to recognize the picture. He was just finishing with another customer.

"Can we pull him into the office to talk?" asked Jeff. "It shouldn't take long."

"Sure," said Kim, putting the register closed sign on the belt. She turned to another employee and asked them to open their register.

"Am I in trouble?" asked the cashier, his face ashen. He looked at all of them. Jeff hated this part; good people being afraid of law officers. He smiled at the young man.

"No," smiled Kim, "you aren't in trouble. You just may be able to help the sheriff."

"I just have a few questions," he said, as gently as possible.

"Okay," said the young man, brightening at the prospect. The four of them walked into the small office and shut the door.

"We are looking for a woman who may be in danger," said Jeff, as the young man sat in a chair and looked at him with expectation. "You thought this woman looked familiar to you when I showed you the picture at your register. Can you take a good look and tell me for sure?" he asked, showing him the picture on his phone screen. The young man leaned forward and studied the picture carefully, then began nodding his head vigorously.

"Yes!" he said excitedly, "she was at my register about half an hour ago!"

"Are you sure?" Jeff asked. The young man nodded again. "Do you remember anything about what this woman bought? Did she say anything at all about where she was going?" asked Jeff anxiously.

"I remember her because she bought hot cocoa mix and I asked her if she wanted marshmallows for the cocoa. She was real pretty, too," he said. Suddenly, he flushed and looked at his bosses. "I mean, she was easy to remember." He looked down at his hands.

"It's alright," said Mike, exchanging a smile with Kim. "You are being helpful." The young man looked relieved and smiled at them, then turned back to Jeff.

"What else do you remember?" asked Jeff.

"Let me think a minute," said the cashier. He closed his eyes and concentrated. "She bought jugs of water, a pan, protein bars…and the hot cocoa! She also bought a cooler." He opened his eyes and smiled, "Did that help?"

"Yes," said Jeff, glancing at Kim and Mike, "you have already helped a lot." By the things she bought, Jeff knew she probably planned to camp somewhere for a few days. There was no use in wasting time checking the motels.

"Did she say anything about going camping?" asked Jeff, just to cover the bases. He was thinking she wouldn't need a pan if she was going to sneak back home or go to a motel somewhere.

"No, she didn't say anything about camping." The cashier scrunched up his face. "She seemed in a hurry to get out of the store; she wasn't very chatty."

"Thank you, you have been very helpful," he said to all of them. He walked outside and called Bodie again. "What did you find out from Scotty's?" he asked.

"She bought a tarp, rope, and a headlamp," he said. "It was easy to get the information, they knew her."

Jeff told Bodie what had transpired at Grocery Outlet. "I have a bad feeling about this Bodie. "

"Something will break," said Bodie. "Someone had to see something! "

"Yeah, but she is as stubborn as they come, and she sure isn't listening to me!" He thought for a minute. "I'm coming back in, we need to look at that map again." He put the phone back on his belt and got in the car. He had a terrible sense of foreboding. He couldn't shake the feeling that someone was going to die soon. He hoped it wasn't Susanna.

# Chapter 13

Susanna looked at her map and then at the mountain in front of her. She remembered the place where she and the sheriff had come down to his Jeep, and found the road on the map where she had left her car. Looking on the other side of the mountain, she found another road that led to an area on the opposite side from where she had seen the men stealing the artifacts.

She started her car again and drove very slowly until she came to a dirt road that seemed to lead in the direction she wanted. She crept along the dirt road, not wanting to raise a cloud of dust that might be seen by observant eyes, friendly or otherwise.

"Who are you kidding?" she said aloud. "Right about now, I'd be willing to bet any eyes looking for me would be hostile!" She chuckled, thinking of how red Jeff's face had been as she drove away. She hoped he didn't find her for a few days, so he could calm down. She was certain he would not be physically violent, but still, she did not want to face a tongue lashing from him when he was angry.

Her eyes scanned the road and the brush around it. It was getting dark now, and she needed to find a sheltered place to park the car and camp for the night. Then she saw the indentation off the side of the road, a low brush area that ended at a stack of boulders. She drove her car carefully over the sparse brush and pulled up behind some trees that formed a wind break. She backed the car into the space, just in case she needed to leave in a hurry. There was a small stand of aspen in front of a grouping of pines, and she loved the way the aspens whispered with the breeze.

She would be hidden from the road, nestled between the trees and the stack of boulders that curved around slightly. She should be safe here, unless someone guessed she might be there, or they were looking for her. But still, she reasoned, no one should expect her to be there, so it should be a good place at least for the night.

She parked the car and got out, looking carefully around. There was a low circle of rocks near the base of the stack of boulders, and just a few feet from her car. It would be a good place for a small fire, which would be shielded by the rocks and her car. She reassured herself again; this would do for tonight.

Susanna walked around to stretch her legs and make sure of her surroundings. She quickly scaled the lower stack of boulders and surveyed the area. Visibility was good, and as far as she could see, there was no sign of movement or recent activity.

Hopping down from the boulders, she gathered some small pieces of dry wood from the base of the nearby stands of trees. It would be enough for a small fire. Susanna popped the trunk and took out her camp shovel. Picking a spot near the boulders, in the corner of the rocks, she dug out a small hole, then lined the rim with a few small rocks laying near the mound of rocks that towered over her. She laid the fire in the pit, then unloaded her tarp, pan, a camping mug, an old hot mitt, and a jug of water. She used the rope and some rocks to secure the tarp and created a type of roof with open sides. It would provide greater shelter, and help shield the light of the fire from anyone who might be looking.

Settling down between her car and the boulders, which formed a rough three sides of a square, she set two rocks a few inches apart on the side of the small pit. Carefully, she lit the fire and watched as it caught the small kindling and started licking at the small pieces of wood. When the fire was burning well, she set the pan on the two rocks she had prepared near the edge of the pit. She poured enough water in the pan to make herself a cup of hot cocoa and a package of instant chicken noodle soup. This is comfort food, she thought. I hope it works.

Susanna hugged her knees as she waited for the water to boil. She always found staring into a camp fire to be soothing. She realized this was the first time in days she had really been alone. It was both comforting and frightening. It was a relief to be alone with her thoughts, and she definitely needed time to think things through. REWRITE

It seemed as if everyone had a say in her life but her, the past couple of days. The men she had seen wanted to kill her, and that kept her in fear. Chris told her she couldn't even open a window, and for a woman who loved to be in the fresh air, that had been tough. Jeff pretty much decided what she could and couldn't do and the time she could do anything. She sighed.

She wished she had never seen those men. As much as she hated the thought of Washoe treasures being stolen and used for personal profit, she wished Jeff had caught them without her involvement. She rubbed her temples, and tried to think.

The boiling water caught her attention, and she took a packet of cocoa and poured it into the camp mug she always carried in her trunk. She poured the water into the mug, stirring it carefully, then set the mug down near the fire, to stay warm. Next, she pulled open the packet of soup and poured it in the remainder of the hot water in the pan. She set the pan down and let the noodles simmer while she dug out a small packet of crackers.

She picked up the pan of soup by the handle that had cooled, and settled it on top of the hot mitt on her lap. She took the spoon out of the cup of cocoa and licked it clean, then began to eat the noodles. She hadn't had much appetite the past few days, so she didn't know if it was the fresh air of freedom or the cumulative effect of so little food intake, but she savored the crackers and noodles and soon emptied the pan. Pouring a little water in the pan, she rinsed it out, then put it back in the ice chest in the trunk area in the back of the car. Between the trunk area and the wall of the ice chest, she was hoping to be able to keep the bears from being attracted by any food smell.

Susanna settled down to look around the edge of the tarp at the stars. Sipping her hot cocoa, she gazed up at the clear night sky, picking out the constellations. This was one of the things she loved about Tahoe, there were no bright masses of city lights to obscure the beauty of the night sky.

A rustle in the bushes on the other side of the road

snapped her back to earth as she struggled to stay calm and try to see what had made the noise. She was questioning her decision to run away from protection when a rabbit hopped out of the brush and sat, staring at her for several minutes. The long eared hare turned back to the bush as three smaller bunnies appeared behind her. The fluffle of rabbits hopped rapidly away and Susanna smiled.

Most people didn't think of rabbits when they thought of the wildlife in the Tahoe area, but the Washoe had made good use of the small mammals, both to eat and to provide warm winter coats and blankets of rabbit pelts, sewn together. They had a ceremonial hunt every fall, with some beating drums and bushes to drive the rabbits to the waiting hunters. Native Americans were very good at making use of nearly everything that came their way, and animals were no exception. They used the bones to make tools, arrowheads, spear heads, needles, and more. The sinew from animals was stretched to make bow strings, thread, and some larger pieces were used like rope. Hard to believe, looking at those little bunnies.

A coyote howled and Susanna drew her jacket closer around her. She had not yet decided whether to sleep outside on the ground or curl up in her car. Ordinarily, she would have stretched her sleeping bag out on the ground and gone to sleep with the brilliant stars overhead and the soft breeze on her cheek, but, she had to admit, she was still a little jumpy.

She sat for another hour, listening to the sounds of the mountain: owls hooting, a bat flying by, another coyote howling, or was it the same one? She tried to sort out her thoughts, thinking of what she really needed to get done for her job, assessing the level of danger with the men still looking for her, and then she thought of Jeff.

She could not figure him out; he wasn't like any other man she had known. One minute he was tough and strong, then he did something thoughtful, like setting up the meeting with Dinah. He even seemed sensitive when she was having a meltdown. But, just when she started to let her guard down and decided he could be trusted, he was all business and making her decisions for her. She shook her head. Suddenly, she felt very tired. She didn't want to think about any of this any longer.

Susanna hesitated for another few minutes, then sighed as she picked up the shovel to put out the fire. She put her mug inside the cooler in the trunk area, and then looked at the box of garbage bags. Just for good measure, she opened the box and took out a bag, which she worked up around the little cooler. She twisted the end and then used a tie to keep it shut. The last thing she needed was a bear coming to say hello in the middle of the night.

Climbing into the back seat of the car, she pulled the sleeping bag around her and settled a pillow against the door. She clicked the key fob and locked all the doors. She hated being scared.

---

The eyes watching her movements from the other side of the shrubs waited several more minutes before slouching away. He thought she might discover him when he startled the four rabbits out of the bushes onto the road. Ten feet further, and he stood upright and walked another twenty yards to his car. He opened the door quietly, slid behind the wheel, and pulled the door shut until it clicked. He had shut off the dome light before he got out of the car earlier.

Sound carried out here, and even though he had left her tucked inside her own car with the windows rolled up, he didn't want to take a chance that she would hear the car and run. He turned the key in the ignition and the engine purred to life softly. Carefully, he crept forward, glad he had backed the car in when it was still light outside. He crawled down the road with just the running lights until he thought it safe to turn on the head lights. He glanced at his phone and saw he had a signal, so he eased the car off the road and hit a button on the phone.

"This better be good!" snarled the man who picked up on the other end.

"I have her, Boss," said Gary. "She is all tucked in for the night in her car, pulled off the road, on the other side of the mountain from our site." Silence greeted this sharing of information. "Boss?" he asked, taking the phone away from his ear for a second to look at the face of the phone, not sure if the connection had dropped.

"I heard you!" snapped the man Gary knew only as the Boss. He had never given them any other name to use. "Shut up, I'm thinking!" he hissed.

Gary sat quietly. He knew better than to say anything else; he knew he was expected to wait until the Boss was damn well ready to talk.

He really needed to find another job. The pay was good, but the Boss was a nasty, demanding, jerk. Gary knew the Boss was a little afraid of him, but that did not make him any more comfortable. Afraid or not, if the right opportunity arose, the Boss would have no qualms about shooting him and dumping his body in a ravine or over a cliff, just like he did to the college kid and Gordy.

"Where are you?" bellowed the Boss into the phone, so loud Gary instinctively moved it away from his ear.

"I'm about a mile down the road from her camp, he replied. "There's only one road in and out here." Silence again.

"How far are you from the entrance to the road?" he growled.

"About another half mile," replied Gary.

"Then get out to the end of the road and make sure she doesn't get away!" He grumbled something Gary didn't understand.

"I'm sorry Boss, you broke up. Was there something else?"

"Yes, you idiot, I said I will be out in the morning and you better not lose her!"

"I won't," he replied. A loud click sounded in his ear and he knew the Boss had hung up.

"Asshole doesn't remember I have a tracking device on her car," he said to himself. He sighed and connected the phone back to the charger.

He drove the car out to the main road, turned around so he was facing the entrance to the side road, and stopped the car. He got out and went to the trunk, where he removed a sleeping bag and walked back to the driver's side of the car. He opened the door and threw the sleeping bag over on the passenger side. He would sleep in the driver's side so he could move quickly if he had to follow her, but he would pull it over him like a blanket. The mountains got cool at night, even in the summer. He hadn't brought a jacket, but he should be warm enough with the sleeping bag.

He shut the front door of the car, and opened the back door. Reaching in, he took out a small cooler and a thermos. He took a sub sandwich out of the cooler and set the wrapped item on the hood of the car. Then he opened the thermos and poured a cup of coffee into the cap. He hesitated a moment, thinking of the flask of Johnny Walker Blue Label he had in the glove compartment, but decided he better not chance getting too relaxed. He liked a good whiskey; it was one of the few comforts he allowed himself. He kept it handy for when he needed a nip, but he didn't dare tonight.

He stood, eating the sandwich and sipping the coffee. It was a beautiful night. What the hell was he doing in the middle of nowhere stalking a girl? He was half tempted to get in the car and drive as far away as he could.

# Chapter 14

Jeff was worried. He finally gave up and rose just as the sun was peeking over the tops of the mountains. He hadn't slept well, even though he was in his own bed last night. He showered and dressed quickly while the coffee was brewing, then filled a thermal cup, and got in the car.

He sipped his morning coffee as he drove, his eyes constantly scanning the streets, the surrounding businesses and homes, and the forest. He had not even taken the time to sit or have breakfast before hitting the streets.

The anger had worn off and now he was just frustrated and concerned. He had tossed and turned all night. None of his officers had seen her, and they had expanded the alert to the surrounding law enforcement entities shortly after she gave him the slip. On second thought, Jeff had Marty send the information to the fire agencies as well. They were always driving around checking on combustible fuels, and they could see something valuable to the search.

Nobody had seen anything. It was as if she disappeared right after she left Grocery Outlet. Where could she have gone? Where had she spent last night? Was she already dead? The thought crept into his mind unannounced and uninvited, and sent a chill down his spine. He clenched his jaw and shook it off. He couldn't let that happen!

He dreaded the thought that she might have fallen into the hands of the thieves. They had proven they could, and would, kill. His thoughts ran through the information they had gathered on the case so far.

Further investigation into the first man they found came back with disturbing information. He was a young college student, who had just completed his Associate of Arts degree, and had decided to hike the Pacific Crest Trail the summer before he went off to a four year college. He had been raised in the basin and was described by friends and family as being gregarious, considerate and kind. He was not carrying a lot of money, and what he had was still in the backpack when they found the body. He had plans to become a teacher. What a shame. It appeared he had been killed just for the thrill, or he had been in the wrong place at the wrong time. Jeff leaned towards the latter, which made these men all the more dangerous as far as Susanna was concerned. These men were ruthless, and had shown no qualms about killing.

He drove the streets, trying to think of some small thing that might give him a clue, but he couldn't shake the feeling that she went back to the mountain. But what area? It was huge. He drove back to her house, and got out. He walked around the exterior, but there was no sign that anyone had been there since she jumped out the window and ran. There were no fresh footprints, no lights on in the house, and the tire marks in the driveway were dry.

He still had a key, which he had kept after the locks had been changed, in case he had to come back and pick something up for her while she was in the safe house. He planned to give it back to her after they caught the men threatening her. The only times he had ever been in her house, she had been with him.

It felt somehow wrong to go in her home without her permission. But if there was any chance it could save her life, if he found even a small clue as to where she went it would be worth it. He hesitated, then stepped to the front door and put the key in the lock. He stepped in quickly and stood still, listening for any sound or indication someone was in the house.

"Susanna?" he said quietly. If she had spent the night here, he didn't want to scare her. There was no sound. No covers being thrown off, no gasp, no light step, nothing. He moved through the house, checking every room and closet. There was no indication that anyone had been in the house since yesterday.

He stood in the middle of her living room, Where could she be? Suddenly, a thought struck him and he slammed his palm against the door.

"No," he said, shaking his head, "she wouldn't be that stupid!" He hoped he was wrong, but he needed to find out. He dialed Bodie.

"What's up, Sheriff?" asked a sleepy voice. Jeff glanced at the time on his phone. It was five fifty in the morning. He grimaced.

"I'm sorry Bodie, I didn't realize the time. I couldn't sleep and I just dialed without looking at the time." Bodie was a good man and he did not want to take advantage of him.

"It's alright, really. I know you wouldn't call unless it was important. I'd be getting up soon anyway." Jeff could hear him stifle a yawn on the other end of the phone. "How can I help?"

"Have we heard anything about Susanna?" asked Jeff.

"No, nobody has reported seeing her," answered Bodie. There was a slight pause, then Bodie spoke. "Have you seen something, boss?"

"No," answered Jeff slowly, "just a hunch, and I really hope I am wrong."

" What are you thinking, boss?" asked Bodie, sounding more awake now.

"I'm thinking she went back to the mountain." Saying it out loud made a shiver run up his spine. There was silence at the other end of the line for a few seconds.

"Damn," said Bodie. "Normally, I would say she wouldn't be that foolish, but this one is really stubborn."

"Yeah, that is the truth!" agreed Jeff. "Listen, Bodie, I wanted you to know what I was thinking because I am going to head up that way and see if I can find any sign of activity. Put our people on alert in case I need help in a hurry."

"You got it, boss, but..." he hesitated.

"What is it, Bodie?" asked Jeff.

"You are the boss and all, but I gotta tell you...," he stopped for a minute. "If I don't hear from you by noon today, a couple of us are gonna come looking for you," Bodie asserted with a touch of bravado Jeff had rarely seen in the man. Jeff smiled.

"Sounds like solid police work to me, Bodie. If I don't call in by noon, I will likely be grateful knowing help is on the way."

"Ok, if I hear anything, I will let you know."

They hung up and Jeff went out Susanna's front door, making sure it was locked behind him.   He climbed in his car and checked the gas tank. It was half full, so he headed towards the nearest gas station. It wouldn't do to get out in the forest and end up on empty.

While he was waiting for the gas to finish pumping, his mind was calculating. He decided to take a look around the area where he first found her to see if he could spot any sign of her. Had she gone back to the same place? Or, he suddenly thought, would she go to a different site in the same area and hope she wouldn't run into the thieves?

# Chapter 15

Susanna woke early the next morning, and experienced the pleasure of a Sierra sun rise in all its glory as it crested the mountain behind her, turning the world around her a beautiful, golden picture.

She climbed out of her car, and stretched herself into the morning, much like the coming day. Inhaling the pure, cool mountain air, she noted the stark blue of the sky, the rich green of the trees, and a few wildflowers, opening their petals to the sun's rays. The granite rock around her shimmered and sparkled in the sun, as the light hit the particles of quartz, feldspar and mica.

"There is nothing like a sunrise in the mountains," she said to herself, as she reached into her pack for a protein bar. She poured herself a cup of water from one of the jugs, and stood, surveying the area once again, in full daylight. She finished her light breakfast and put her cup back in the vehicle.

A dark spot on the mountain caught her interest and she studied it carefully. She hadn't noticed it in the fading light last night, but today, it held her attention. The Washoe were not known as cave dwellers, but still, there could be something close.

She debated on whether to move her car or leave it. She ultimately decided it would be safer to have it close, so she quickly dismantled her make shift camp, packed everything in the car, and began to drive slowly towards what she believed was a cave.

Almost directly below the spot on the mountain, she found a large stand of pine trees, surrounding a semi circle of open meadow. Looking towards the center of the meadow, she saw several fairly flat rocks, clustered in the middle. She would explore those later to see if they were grinding rocks, but right now, she backed her car into a space between the trees. It wasn't very secluded, and her car could be seen fairly easily if anyone were around, but it would have to do for now.

She took her pack out again and checked it for basic first aid supplies, and made sure her small field kit was in the pack.

Her grandfather had taught her the importance of being prepared for the unexpected, and it had become an ingrained habit to check her supplies before she set out in the field. If she did find something, she might need more than the camera function on her phone. She put her phone in the side snap pocket of the back pack, then put her headlamp in the pack. Her compass was in her pocket, along with her car keys, and she slipped her water bottle in the side pocket of her pack. She hesitated, then grabbed another protein bar and threw it in the pack as well.

Susanna started off at a fast clip, feeling good about getting some exercise after being cooped up for a couple of days. She reached the bottom of the mountain, and began picking her way up the slope, boulder hopping, and pushing through some small brush.

At least she didn't have to worry about rattlesnakes at this elevation. The warm blooded reptiles did not like the cold temperatures up on the mountain. Even in the summer, the night time temperature could drop into the thirties, and snow had been experienced every month of the year, even on the fourth of July.

It took her the better part of two hours to get up to the opening, where she stopped on a small ledge outside the cave. She caught her breath as a chipmunk skittered across the trail in front of her, then stopped and stood on its hind legs several feet from her. The small rodent proceeded to cheep loudly at her, in the voice they use to defend their territory. She smiled at the tiny beast clucking in a high pitch at a regimented interval.

"I'm not here to stay, little buddy," she laughed, "I'm just going to look around, and then I'll be on my way!" But as her gaze shifted beyond him, her smile froze on her face. She walked forward carefully until she stood full in front of the rock. It was turned toward the East, and therefore, she had not seen it from the bottom of the mountain. It was only when she stood on the ledge, that she could see the recessed rock.

The images chipped into the rock were clearly Native American, and very likely Washoe. She did not touch the rock, but studied it carefully, with building euphoria. This is what she was looking for when she came back to this area! There was a gathering basket on the rock, and that made her turn to look again at the rocks in the meadow below. The proximity of the stand of trees to the rocks in the meadow, and the image of the gathering basket on the rock, could be an indication this was an area where the Washoe gathered pine cones to bake in the sun, so the nuts could be harvested. From the high vantage point, she could see the tree line stretched much further than she originally thought.

Her excitement grew as she looked beyond the rocks in the meadow. She could clearly see some kind of large rock circle, where they would have put the pine cones after transporting them to the area.

She turned back to the rock in front of her and noted another, smaller rock next to the first one. On this, were drawn two concentric circles, one larger than the other, one higher than the other. Concentric circles are found in the rock art of many Native American tribes, but the meaning may vary according to tribe. They are all symbolic of some sort of life process, like a shaman leaving the earth or a symbol of life in an area. Some of the Washoe elders believed the concentric circle was a symbol of life.

What did it mean that it was here, in this place? This could be where she could find proof the Washoe had been here too. She set her pack down and took out her phone. Then she took careful pictures of the rock, and the open area stretching out below her.

Susanna turned her attention back to the mouth of the cave. She took her headlamp out of her back pack and secured the strap around her head, flipping on the switch that gave out a bright, steady light. She stepped to the mouth of the cave and shone her light into the darkness, moving slowly from one side of the cave to the other. Cautiously, she moved into the cave, examining the ground carefully before each step.

A small grouping of rocks in the center of the cave, a few feet from the entrance, brought her to her knees. Without touching them, she decided they were probably the remnants of a small fire ring. Moving her head slowly, she fanned out to the wall of the cave opposite the camp fire site. Something small and white was barely visable beneath the dirt.

Moving carefully, she came up to the small white object. Taking a field kit out of her backpack, she removed a small brush. She began slowly brushing the dirt from the object until she could see its shape. It was a claw from an animal; it appeared to be from a bear. One claw? From a bear? Bears were sacred animals to the Washoe.

She continued to check the cave, and found a scratched sign of the circle again, and what looked like a man, lying down. This was definitely something she needed to report. She took more pictures, unwilling to disturb in any other way the site until she could document everything in minute detail. Carefully, she made her way to the mouth of the cave again.

Standing outside once more, she moved along the ledge as far as she could, looking for more signs the Washoe had been here. She sat on the ledge and sketched the area, creating her own map of the points she wanted to explore more thoroughly. She decided to go down the mountain at a different spot, one that would bring her closer to the rock circle. She was back in her element; this was what she was born to do.

---

Gary woke early the next morning, and after packing his sleeping bag back in the trunk, he stood outside and had another cup of coffee from the big thermos. It was still warm, but not hot, and he wrinkled his nose at the coolness of the coffee as he swallowed. He liked his coffee hot.

He started to take another sip, thinking that coffee was still coffee, when he suddenly stopped. Smiling, he set down the cup on the hood of the car and reached into the glove compartment for his flask. The coffee might be cold, but a generous portion of the Jonnie Walker Blue Label whiskey would certainly make it warmer as it slid down his throat.

His stomach growled, and he wished he had thought to bring another sandwich for breakfast. Well, he would go check on the girl, then call the Boss. Maybe someone would relieve him or bring him at least a breakfast burrito from Jalapenos. His mouth watered at the thought of their bacon, potato, cheese, and egg burrito. Or, maybe a toasted cheese bagel and cream cheese from Don's Cakes by the Lake Bake Shop. Yeah, he was hungry!

He slid behind the wheel of the car and started the engine. Slowly, he eased back down the road to the spot he parked last night and got out of the car. He crept forward slowly, paying attention to any wildlife he might disturb. He was lucky last night, but it could be his downfall in the morning light. She would be more alert and he would be easier to see.

He decided he would cross the road and come up behind her, around the mass of rock, where it would be harder to see him approach. It took a little longer, but he finally came to the end of the grouping of boulders. He scaled the rock soundlessly and rose slowly to peek over the top.

When he did, he almost lost his footing. She was gone! She couldn't have slipped out in the night, could she? No, he told himself, that would have been impossible. He looked up the road, but he did not see her vehicle.

Gary quickly climbed down off the rocks and slipped around the side to where he had last seen her. The tire tracks in the soft sand told the story, and he followed them out to the road, where they turned left. She had gone further in. That was a good thing for them. There was only one road in and the same road out on this part of the mountain.

He smiled to himself and walked back to his car. He drove back out until he got a signal, then made his call.

"If you lost her, you're a dead man!" barked the Boss in his ear as the phone was answered. Gary clenched his teeth. He was beginning to hate the Boss.

"Good morning, Boss," he said a little too sweetly. The sarcastic tone was lost on the Boss.

"Where is she, you piece of shit!"

"She drove back in a little further this morning, so now she is really trapped," replied Gary.

"Good! It's time to take this bitch out and bury her in the forest where they will never find her!" He could hear the Boss yell for Juan. "We'll be there in less than half an hour. Meet us by the road in."

"Uh, Boss, could someone bring me something to eat? I'm starving." The loud click in his ear answered his question. Gary swore at the phone, then plugged it in again. His stomach was really growling. He dug through the console, and found an old peppermint hard candy. He didn't know how long it had been there and he didn't care. He removed the wrapper and popped it in his mouth. Maybe it would at least be enough to stop his stomach from making noises.

# Chapter 16

Jeff drove quickly to the road that had brought him closer to the thieves the day he met Susanna. Half of him wanted her to be here, so he could find her before they did. Half of him wanted her to be on the other side of the mountain, where, he hoped, she was safe.

He turned onto the road and drove about a half mile before he parked off on the side. He got out of the Jeep, and grabbed his water bottle. He took a healthy drink, then put it back in the jeep. He didn't want to be slowed down with extra weight.

He unclipped the strap on his holster that held his gun in place. He withdrew the Sig Sauer P226 from the holster and by habit, checked the magazine to make sure it still held fifteen rounds. He preferred the increased accuracy of the slightly longer barrel on this hand gun. If he had to shoot someone, he wanted to make sure his shots went where they were intended. He put two more, fully loaded magazines in his pockets. Jeff had no illusions about the men he was dealing with out here; they were cold blooded killers. His life, and Susanna's, could depend on how prepared he was for a gun fight.

He started up the mountain at a different angle than he had before, and climbed rapidly under the heavy cover of the trees. Nearly an hour later, he came to the spot where he had thrown Susanna to the ground to save her from the shotgun blast. He stopped and listened carefully. He heard nothing, except the squawk of a Stellar Jay and the chatter of a squirrel.

He moved carefully forward, stopping every few feet to listen, and look around the area. It was so quiet, it was almost eerie. He came to the edge of the clearing where he had first seen Susanna. He listened, but heard nothing.

He scanned the edges of the clearing and saw rock debris, but no people. He finally stepped into the open space and looked around. He could see trash and rocks strewn around the area, and deep ruts in the ground where a heavily loaded pick up trunk or small utility truck had driven away. It was a tight squeeze, but they had made it into and out of this area.

He noted indentations in the ground where boulders had been. There was black residue on the surrounding boulders, indicating there had been a blast of some sort. He saw a mass of rock in a heap near a large boulder and walked over to it. A huge boulder stood beside the mound of broken rock, its face nearly sheered off. Jeff looked at it closely.

"Seems like they tried to use a pneumatic chisel on this rock," he said to a chipmunk watching him. "It appears they tried to cut this face off in one big sheet." He knelt and looked more closely at the pile of rubble on the ground. He picked up one larger piece and discovered it held part of a petroglyph. "Damn it," he said with disgust. He placed the piece back on the ground and stood, shaking his head.

They had both destroyed and stolen precious artifacts from this area. They had killed and they had destroyed sacred history. He wanted these men, and he wanted them bad.

Susanna was not here. He began the descent of the mountain, and was back at the Jeep in about forty-five minutes. He started the vehicle and swung it around to go back the way he came. He had to find her. He prayed she was on the other side of the mountain and she was still safe.

---

Gary watched as the Boss got out of the car and advanced on him. The Boss had sunken eyes that shot meanness out of them every time Gary had seen him. The dark circles around his eyes seemed to have darkened in recent days, giving him a look that was almost macabre. His shoulders were slightly stooped and his hands were clenched at his sides.

Juan, and a new guy Gary recognized from an old job, got out and stood behind the Boss.

"Where is she?" growled the Boss. His scowl made him look even older. Gary knew he drank heavily, and hoped he didn't smell the whiskey on Gary's own breath.

"She's down this road about a mile and a half," Gary said, hooking his thumb over his shoulder.

"Well, what are you waiting for? Get your ass in the car and lead the way!" He stomped back to the car and got in, slamming the door. Juan and Neil started to follow him.

"Hey, Juan?" Gary said. Juan turned.

"Yeah Gary?" Juan replied.

"Did you guys bring me anything to eat?" Gary looked at Juan. "I told the Boss I was starving and asked him to have one of you guys pick up something before you came out here."

"Naw man, I'm really sorry," he said, and looked like he meant it. Juan was another kid Gary hoped would get out before he ended up like Gordy. "I woulda grabbed something if I'd known." He turned and got back in the car with the Boss and Neil in the front.

Gary glanced at the Boss, who was glaring at him from the front seat of the car. Gary got back in his own car and started it up. He eased on down the road. The Boss was just pure poison. And now, Neil was in the mix.

Gary didn't like or trust Neil. He had worked with him on another job where he beat a man to death and then raped and beat the man's girlfriend. Gary had come back too late to save the man, but he pulled Neil off the woman before he killed her. It had been Gary who drove her to the emergency room, and left her sitting on a bench outside where she would be found.

He kept on driving when he drove away from the hospital; he never went back to that job.

"That's what I should do right now," he said to the empty car. He slowed as he came up to the area where he had parked before. He pulled off and stopped, then got out of the car and waited for them to pull in behind him. He walked over to the window by the Boss.

"Well?" he demanded.

"She camped right up there last night," he said, pointing up the road, "by that stack of boulders. But, I don't know for sure that she didn't come back. I think we should walk from here, at least until we are sure."

"Oh you do, huh?" The Boss curled his lip. "Well, I think you ought to earn your pay and get your ass up the road and find her before we all go walking!"

Gary stared at the Boss for a minute, then nodded and turned away. He started walking up the road, but quickly moved into the brush. It was slower going, but if she saw him coming and got away, he knew he had no future.

He walked for about a half hour before he looked up and saw her. She was sitting on a ledge, about a hundred feet up the side of the mountain. She was sketching something, and was not looking in his direction. He looked around, but could not see what was holding her interest. He did not see her car, but knew it must be close.

Gary turned and moved away slowly, afraid to move quickly as he knew sometimes that could draw the human eye towards the movement. When he could no longer see her, he moved fast to get back to the Boss.

The Boss was pacing back and forth as Gary approached. He stopped, his hands balled into fists on his hips, and glared as Gary came closer.

"Where the hell have you been?" he demanded. Gary bit his tongue to hold back what he wanted to say.

"If I moved too fast, I could have scared her away," he said. "Is that what you want?" he pushed. He knew he was on dangerous ground, but he was tired, he was hungry, and he was sick of the bad moods of the Boss. The Boss took a step towards him, pointing his finger at Gary's chest.

"Maybe we should get going before she gets away," said Juan, sending a look of understanding in Gary's direction. The Boss whirled on him and started to speak, then changed his mind.

"Get moving!" he hissed at Gary. He did not like having the Boss or Neil behind him, but he had no choice right now. He glanced behind him and noticed Juan was bringing up the rear. Their eyes met for a second and Juan nodded almost imperceptibly, but Gary got it. At least he would get a warning if anything was coming his way.

He picked his way forward, changing direction slightly to be closer to the base of the mountain. Suddenly, he held up his hand. He could still see her sitting on the ledge, only now, she seemed to be eating something. His stomach growled again.

"Is that her?" hissed the Boss in his ear. His breath stank of beer and Gary had to turn his head to grab some fresh air.

"Yeah," said Gary, nodding his head.

"Why don't we go get her?" said the Boss. Gary looked at him briefly.

"Because she is about a hundred feet above us," said Gary. "She isn't just going to come down because we ask her."

"I'm getting tired of your smart ass mouth," said the Boss.

"Well, I'm tired and I'm hungry, let me think!" snapped Gary. This time the Boss looked at him, started to speak, then shut his mouth and nodded. Gary was still the best man he had, and he knew it, even though he didn't like to admit it.

Gary crept back to Juan and Neil, and the Boss followed. Gary was still eyeing the slope of the mountain.

"Juan, do you think you can get up the slope off to the right of where she is sitting?" asked Gary.

"Yeah," said Juan, searching the slope, "it looks like there is a way to traverse that slope right over to that ledge." He studied the rocks and brush on the slope. "What are you thinking?"

"I'm thinking if you come at her from the right and Neil goes up the left..."

"I don't take my orders from you!" sneered Neil. Gary locked eyes with him and started to speak, but was interrupted.

"Do what he says!" said the Boss, hitting him with a harsh look. "We don't have time for a pissing match!"

"If Neil goes up the slope to the left," continued Gary, "I think we can frighten her into coming down the slope." He looked at Neil. "You'll have to go over to the right at the base of the mountain, and hug the side as you try to get past her and come up on her left without being seen," he said. "Even if she sees you coming up, if she sees Juan coming across towards her, she may try to come straight down between you," he said.

"Where we will be waiting," chuckled the Boss. "You finally have a good idea!" Get going," he snapped, focusing on Juan and Neil. The two men began moving rapidly.

---

Susanna had her eyes closed, enjoying the sun on her face and the sweet smell of sage on the soft breeze. She was exhilarated! She was certain she had found something significant and could not wait to get down off the mountain and send notice to her supervisor, Rebecca, at the Smithsonian.

Susanna looked down towards the circle of rocks and then started to stand. Movement to her right caught her eye, and she found herself staring into the eyes of a man she had never seen. He leered at her, and put a dirty hand out to the next rock to pull himself towards her. His clothes were filthy and his hair looked as if it hadn't been washed in weeks.

Her hand went to her throat, and she took a step backward. Who was this man, who was coming at her with a deliberate purpose? She turned suddenly to go back across the ledge to the cave. Another man was coming across the slope from her left, only she recognized this one. He was one of the men she had seen that first day; one of the men stealing the petroglyphs! She had to get away!

Susanna grabbed her pack and started down the slope between the two men. This was not the route she had taken to get up to the top, but it was her only choice to avoid the men. If she could get to the bottom before they caught up, she might get to her car and get away. She risked a look back over her shoulder, and saw them reach the top and start down after her. She went faster, but hesitated when a talus slope opened up before her. She turned sideways and started down the slope; knowing it could slide from under her at any time. Talus slopes were very unstable. Descending sideways with one leg extended in front of her and one bent to the side would help her balance.

Suddenly the slope shifted and she felt herself sliding fast. She leaned over more towards the mountain to keep her balance. She was sliding towards the bottom and was more than half way down, when her foot caught on a tree root and flipped her on her side. She grabbed frantically for anything to stop her fall, but it was no use. She began to roll over and over. The dust from the shale was choking, and bits of slate cut her hands. She crossed her arm over her face to protect her eyes.

Finally, she came to an abrupt stop as she hit something solid. She opened her eyes and was looking at a small boulder. Her ribs hurt, but she struggled to her knees. She shook her head to clear it and turned to get a leg under her to stand. She had to get to her car.

"Well, well well. Look who just dropped in to the party!" said a voice. "And you brought a present! How nice!"

Susanna knew that voice. Her head snapped up and she found herself looking right into the cold eyes of the man who had been giving the orders at the site of the theft of the artifacts. She screamed, and he threw his head back and laughed. It was not a nice sound.

"No one can hear you out here," he laughed. He leaned over close to her and reached down. "What have we here?" The Boss knelt and picked up a human skull from the ground beside Susanna.

Susanna scrambled to her feet in horror. A human skull in this area was likely to be Washoe! She looked down and saw a shell bead necklace on a worn strip of rawhide. The Washoe sometimes buried their dead with their belongings. She thought of the drawing in the cave.

"Don't touch that!"she said. "It is probably a Washoe burial site. I must have disturbed it when I came down the talus!" She looked at the man and pleaded. "Please, don't do this!"

"It's what we do, nosy bitch!" He hefted the skull in his hands. "People will pay good money for this!"

"No, you can't! It's sacred!" He shoved his face within an

inch of hers.

"I'll do whatever I damn well please, and my men will do what I tell them to do," he said, eyes narrowing. "Take her boys," he said. "Throw her in the trunk until we get her back to the hideout." He grinned at her. "And after you put her in the trunk, pick up any other artifacts or bones you can find!"

Strong hands grabbed her from behind, pinning her arms to her sides. She twisted and screamed again. The dirty man pulled a raunchy cloth from his pocket and a small bottle from the pocket inside his jacket. He tipped the bottle and poured some of the liquid on the dirty cloth. Grinning, he advanced on her and held the cloth over her mouth and nose. She struggled to keep from vomiting as the world went black.

Chapter 17

Jeff whirled as the scream split the air. Where did it come from, which direction? Sound carried here in the clear mountain air, and he struggled to determine the source. Was it Susanna? He was turning around slowly, listening, when the second scream came to his ears.

East! He jumped in his Jeep and headed down the road towards the other side of the mountain. He was caught between going slowly so they would not see his dust and know he was near, or driving quickly to get to her before they hurt her anymore, or took her. It had to be Susanna; it was unlikely another woman would be this far out in the wild.

Scanning the horizon, he suddenly saw dust rising in the sky in front of him. He stepped on the gas; if it was them, he needed to see where they were headed, if not, his dust wouldn't matter. He came around a curve and saw Susanna's car ahead, on the side of the road. He slowed slightly, but did not see any sign of a person in the car, so he accelerated again.

The dust cloud in front of him was receding fast. His eyes traveled frantically across the landscape and the road ahead, but he saw no sign of anyone. He made a decision. He would follow the car at least long enough to determine she was or was not in one of them. If they kept heading in this direction, they could cut across a strip of open land and circle around to a paved road, where it would be easier to see their car. They would also be able to see him, but he had to take that chance.

He glanced at his phone. No service. It was after noon and he hadn't called Bodie. He reached for the Motorola Talkabout MS350R radio on the seat beside him and listened briefly, then pressed the PTT key.

"Prospector One, Prospector One, this is Top Star One, come in, over." He waited, listening for Bodie. Jeff and several of his officers had used the Motorola Talkabout MS350R's in the Angora Fire. They had a range up to thirty-five miles and were far more reliable than cell phone service in an emergency.

There was no response. Jeff glanced at the mountain beside him, wondering if it was blocking the signal. The Talkabouts were very good, but sometimes even their signal could be blocked temporarily by a large, dense obstacle.

They had cut across the open land and he followed. The car in front of him slowed for the turn onto the paved road, and he shortened the gap a little. The dust was abating, and he got a better look, as he too turned onto the paved road. He hit the PTT button again.

"Prospector One, Prospector One, this is Top Star. Come in. Over."

"Top Star One, this is Prospector One. Go ahead. Over." Hearing Bodie's voice swept Jeff with relief.

"Pursuing black Toyota Highlander, License 9 Hotel India Sierra 478." Jeff used the international phonetics code for the alphabet to convey an unspoken message to Bodie that others could be listening, and he did not want them to understand this was a pursuit by law enforcement. He didn't want thrill seekers in the way. "Hwy 89, headed towards Picketts Junction," he continued. May have captured stubborn bird. Over." Jeff hoped Bodie understood the 'stubborn bird' to be Susanna.

"Copy," said Bodie, "requesting more stars in your hat?" Bodie said. They both knew this was not as secure as a radio they might normally use.

"Affirmative. Over."

"Standby," said Bodie. Jeff waited in silence for a few minutes. "Top Star One, this is Prospector One, do you copy?" Bodie was back.

"Copy," said Jeff.

"One green shooting star will connect at Picketts Junction, two more shooting stars in transit. Over," said Bodie.

"Copy that. Might be some prospecting to be done three miles off highway, up dirt road, opposite previous site. Over." Jeff wanted a team to go back to the area where he saw her car, just in case she was there and could be hurt.

"Wilco," responded Bodie, indicating he understood Jeff

wanted him to check the area he had just left.

"Out," said Jeff. The 'shooting green star' was their own code for a game warden. They were usually tough officers, used to being on their own in the middle of nowhere, with the possibility they may run into armed poachers, or worse. He hoped the warden Bodie was talking about was Tom Wilcox, former Army Ranger and a crack shot with a rifle. Jeff and Tom had spent many weekends camping and hiking in the Hope Valley area, and they read each other's thoughts easily.

He gained on the car on the clear pavement and squinted to see inside the car. A face peered back at him, one he thought looked familiar. He did not see Susanna.

---

Juan stared out the back window of the car. He thought he had seen a dust cloud behind them, too far back to be from their own car. Now that they had turned onto the paved road, the dust had dissipated and he could see a green Jeep following behind them.

"Boss, I think we might be followed," said Juan. He was worried. He liked this job less every day. He was a thief, he owned that, but he did not sign on to murder any one. He suspected the Boss had done away with Gordy, even though he couldn't prove it. He read the papers about a young man found dead over the edge of a cliff on the hike to Eagle Falls. The picture was Gordy. He wasn't stupid, even though the Boss thought so. Juan also knew the Boss planned to kill the girl they had in the trunk area. And he did not want any part of that.

"What are you talking about?" snapped the Boss, turning around. Neil looked in the rear view mirror as he drove.

"There's a green Jeep behind us," said Juan, "I think he turned on the road from the dirt road by the mountain."

"What are you smoking, you whiny little scaredy cat?" sneered Neil. "That's a green Game Warden truck, can't you tell the difference?" he taunted. "And we ain't got no game in or on the car," he snickered, "unless you count the doe in the trunk area," he laughed. It was an ugly laugh.

"Sorry, I guess I was wrong," said Juan. He looked out the back window again. He could have sworn it was a green Jeep following them, not a green truck.

---

The black Toyota had just disappeared around a curve in the road when Jeff spotted the green game warden truck pull out of a stand of trees and on to the shoulder. Jeff slowed as he approached and a man leaned out of the window of the truck. Jeff rolled the passenger window down as he pulled up beside the other vehicle.

"Hey Tom!" said Jeff. The game warden nodded at Jeff.

"That your pigeon in the black Toyota?" asked Tom.

"Yeah," said Jeff.

"I'll take point," said Tom, pulling out ahead of Jeff and accelerating rapidly to catch up.

Jeff knew Tom would follow them and keep him informed once they stopped. They would not suspect a game warden following them on a highway in this area. If they went off road, Tom would know where they were going and appear to go a different direction to throw them off. He also knew Tom was a seasoned veteran when it came to combat of any kind. If he only had one man on his side out here, he couldn't ask for anyone better than Tom.

Jeff dropped back so he wouldn't be so easy to spot. He even let another car get between him and Tom at Picketts Junction, where they pulled onto Highway 88, towards Blue Lakes. If Susanna was in that car, they would find her.

## Chapter 18

Susanna could hear the back of the Toyota being opened. Her head hurt and she felt groggy. What had they put on that nasty rag they put over her mouth and nose?

"Get her out of there and bring her inside now!" snapped the Boss.

The blanket was ripped off her and she found herself being lifted out of the back of the Toyota. They had tied her hands after she passed out, and she had to concentrate to keep her balance at first on the uneven ground.

"Careful," said the younger of the two, as her foot rolled on a rock. She looked into the eyes of the dark haired young man she had seen at the site that first day on the mountain. He looked worried, but he was gentle with her. He didn't push or shove her, and while he held her arm firmly, he wasn't rough.

"Watch your step," said the other man beside her. She hadn't seen him before she had landed at the bottom of the slope. He was older, maybe mid forties, with dark brown hair and hazel eyes. He was tall, and looked strong, but he was easy with her as well.

They led her up two steps to the small porch of an old, rough cabin, made of logs and weathered wood. A stack of firewood formed a barrier of sorts just up the steps and on the outside edges of the porch.

Inside, there was a table, two chairs, a cot on one side of the room, and an old bed built into the wall on the other side of the room. The only window in the dimly lit room was in the wall across from the bed. It was shut tight, and the room smelled musty, with old wood smoke and cooking smells lingering in the stale air. A wood stove stood in one corner, with a full wood box a few feet away. It had obviously been recently used to make coffee and something requiring an old cast iron skillet, which still sat on top of the stove.

"Put her over there on the bed," said the Boss, and leave her hands tied."

"Yeah, put her on the bed, Gary," leered the one that had put the nasty rag over her mouth.

"Neil!" warned Gary. "You keep…"

"That's enough!" snapped the one they called Boss. "Juan, go on out and bring in the cooler!" The young man walked outside and Susanna looked around the room. Her heart sank as she suddenly realized they were all using their names. Jeff was right. With a mounting sense of fear, she realized they used the names because they didn't care if she knew. They were going to kill her.

Juan came back in with the cooler, and the Boss walked over, opened it, and took out a beer. He popped the cap and took a long swig, then sat and stared at her. Gary went to the cooler and saw there were several sub sandwiches in the cooler in a plastic bag.

He took one out, unwrapped it quickly, and began to eat rapidly. His eyes came up and met hers, as she watched him. He looked at the sandwich in his hand, then back at her. He tore off an end and walked towards her.

"Are you hungry?" he asked, holding the chunk of sandwich so she could bite pieces off if she leaned forward a little.

"No, thank you," said Susanna.

"You'd just be wasting it on her anyway," said Neil, with an ugly smile.

The Boss laughed, then finished his beer and threw the bottle over by the door. He got up and sauntered over to the cooler, where he took out another beer, took the lid off, and drew a long gulp. He fixed his eyes on Susanna.

"What were you doing up on that ledge?" he asked, his eyes narrowing. Susanna returned his glare. They may kill her, but she wasn't going to help them destroy or steal artifacts or human remains. He took a few steps towards her.

"I said, what were you doing up on that ledge!" He leaned into her face now. Susanna turned her head away from his putrid breath, but he reached out with one big hand and clutched her cheeks hard, forcing her head back towards him. "Answer me!"

he growled. She remained mute.

Suddenly, he grabbed her hair and yanked her head back. He laughed in her face when she gasped, then roughly jerked his hand away, causing her to lose her balance and fall over to her side. Behind the Boss, she saw Juan start forward, but Gary grabbed him and pulled him back, shaking his head in warning. She struggled to sit back up, and when she did, she stared at him in defiance.

"You'll talk," he smiled. "I can wait. Or, I can always let Neil take over." The Boss and Neil exchanged a look and laughed. It sent a chill through Susanna as she watched the two men.

---

Outside the cabin, Jeff and Tom stood in the trees, watching the cabin. The sun was behind the mountain now and dark was closing in.

"I knew where they were headed as soon as they turned down the road, "said Tom. He shifted his tall, lean form against a tree. "This old cabin has been basically deserted since the late 1950's. I keep wondering how it is still standing, but they built them tough back then."

"Almost too strong; it still looks pretty solid," said Jeff. "And we are definitely outnumbered, two to one."

"Oh, I don't know, Mr. Remington here can sure help even the odds," smiled Tom, patting the rifle he held.

"Any ideas on getting them to come out of the cabin?" Jeff asked. "I think that is better than us trying to go in," he said. "Susanna might get hurt if we just break down the door," he added. Tom thought for a minute, then grinned. There was a twinkle in his ice blue eyes as he looked at Jeff.

"Think their car is one of those new ones that honk and flash if you bump it?" he asked.

"Seems so," said Jeff, looking at the fairly new Toyota. He watched as Tom looked around him, then knelt and hefted a few pine cones.

"This one will do," he said, bouncing a big cone in his hand. He took a step forward out of the trees, and lobbed it up in an arch towards the car. It hit the roof of the car with a resounding thud, and true to expectation, the horn starting bleating and the lights started flashing.

———————

Inside the cabin, the Boss whirled sharply as the noise broke the silence around them. "What the hell?" Neil, get out there and see what that is all about!"

Neil reached behind his back and pulled a Beretta out of his waistband. He checked the magazine, then opened the front door cautiously a crack, peering into the descending darkness. After several minutes, he stepped quickly out on the little porch, pulling the door shut behind him, and looked carefully around. He slowly went down the steps, his head swiveling back and forth and both hands on his gun, ready to fire.

He went over to the car and saw the heavy pine cone on the ground. He kicked it away from the car and dug in his pocket for the keys. He turned to hit the key fob and stop the irritating noise.

"Put your hands up and keep your mouth shut," said a voice behind him. Neil froze. "Drop that gun nice and slow," the voice continued. Neil stood, hands in the air, debating what to do. Could he swing around fast enough? Suddenly, the cabin door opened, sending a dim swath of light over them.

"Neil!" yelled the Boss from the door, "what the hell are you doing?" Neil felt the man behind him shift and look for just a minute at the door. Neil took his chance and dropped and rolled, kicking out with his steel toed boot and throwing Tom off balance with the kick to his leg.

The Boss saw the man with the rifle trained on Neil, and drew his gun to shoot. From the distance, he couldn't be sure, but he thought the man with the rifle was wearing a game warden jacket.

Jeff had his eyes on the door when the Boss threw it opened, and as he saw the Boss draw his gun, Jeff fired a warning shot into the door jamb. The Boss immediately jumped to the right and out of the light from the doorway. He crouched behind the stack of wood on the porch and started returning fire in the direction of the woods where Jeff stood, using the tree trunks for cover.

The Boss shifted his gaze to where Neil and the man with the rifle had stood, hoping to fire a shot at the man. But Neil was gone and the man was scrambling around the end of the car. The Boss fired off one shot at the man in the game warden jacket, and then turned his attention back to the stand of trees, where Jeff had been. Where was Neil?

---

At the sound of the first shot, Gary leapt to the door and slammed it shut. He knew it would help the Boss hide in the dark, but he also had his own reasons. He looked at Juan, who was a little pale, then he drew his Swiss Army Knife out of his front pocket and stepped over to Susanna.

"I'm letting her go, Juan," Gary said, half challenge, half assertion. Juan's shoulders sagged in relief.

"You won't get any argument from me," said Juan. "I didn't sign on to be a killer."

"I'm going to cut the rope tying your hands," Gary said to Susanna. He was kneeling beside her now and looked in her eyes. "But you are on your own after that," he said. She nodded. "I'm sorry, we can't help you more than setting you free."

"I understand," replied Susanna.

"And don't waste precious time fighting us," Juan interjected, as if he was afraid she might attack them once she was free. He didn't know how to fight women.

"I just want to get out of here," she said. Gary reached behind her and cut the ropes. He rose immediately and went to the lamp in the room, dousing the light. Susanna could see the window on the far side of the room, with light from the rising moon and stars making it stand out in the dark room. She rubbed her wrists to restore the feeling before she stood.

Gary glanced back in her direction, then drew his gun. With one hand on the door knob and the other on his gun, he opened the door quickly and ducked outside and to the left, behind the wood pile. The Boss turned and saw Juan in the doorway, deep in the shadows.

Gary moved to the far end of the wood pile, and when the next shot came at the location where the Boss was settled, Gary suddenly ran to the end of the short porch and rolled off the edge, then moved to the side of the house.

Juan inched over to crouch in the door way, using the partially closed door for cover. Susanna skittered over to the window. With some effort, she managed to get the old window open, and hearing another volley of gun fire, she quickly went out the window and dropped to the ground beneath.

She hunched beneath the window for a few minutes, listening and trying to get her bearings. Suddenly, she heard more vehicles coming down the road. The gun fire stopped for a few minutes as if they too were trying to decide if the incoming vehicles were friendly or not. She didn't hear any voices or sounds of movement, and uncertain, she hesitated a moment longer. Suddenly, she sprinted in a stooped position to get to the other side of a rock that was about ten feet in front of her. She couldn't wait to find out who was shooting at her captors. For all she knew, it could be a rival gang of thieves.

She ducked behind the large rock and listened. The vehicles had stopped, and she could hear doors slamming.

"Tom! Jeff!" someone called out. Jeff was here, then! She somehow felt a little safer knowing he was in the woods, even though she would rather he was next to her. She did not hear any response to the call, but they may have moved towards the reinforcements without sound until they got close enough to whisper.

Rustling and snapping twigs about five feet to her right frightened her. It was totally dark now. She did not think Jeff was that close. It could be Gary or Juan, but she could not be sure. Carefully, she moved a little further down the slope, away from the rustling she had heard, and towards a big boulder she could see outlined against the sky line. She was moving slowly, trying to be quiet when the air suddenly exploded with the sound of gunfire. She leapt like a scared rabbit and landed behind the boulder, cowering in fear, not knowing whether to stay put or run.

# Chapter 19

Susanna huddled behind the big boulder, trying to sink as low to the ground as possible. She covered her ears against the loud popping, hearing the bullets as they whined off the rocks and slammed into trees. She couldn't see anything. She didn't know where the men were who had abducted her. She didn't know where Jeff was and she didn't know what to do, except that she needed to get away from the cabin, away from her kidnappers. Yet, she was afraid to move.

Suddenly, the choice was made for her as she felt a hard metal tube thrust into her ribs. The foul smell of unwashed clothing and old sweat preceded the hiss of disgusting breath in her ear.

"Crawl backwards until I tell you to stop," he growled. "If you try to run or scream, I will kill you." Susanna slowly crept backward, unable to see where she was going. She tried to get her bearings. For all she knew, he could be inching to the edge of one of the drop offs in this area.

A few yards away, there was the sound of crashing through the brush and the snapping of branches. The man who had her at gun point shoved her down in the dirt.

"Be quiet or else." He whispered roughly. A shot was fired and then more people running through the brush. The steps moved away from them and it grew quiet. An arm clad in a filthy jacket sleeve pressed around her neck.

"We're gonna stand up now," the man whispered, "stay real close to me and don't try anything. She could still feel the gun in her side as she nodded. They rose slowly until they were standing. The man dropped his arm around her waist and suddenly jerked her body hard against his. He pushed against her buttocks and nuzzled his face in her hair. Susanna fought the urge to throw up.

"You're kinda pretty. Maybe we'll have a little fun before I turn you back over to the Boss."

"Don't touch me," she spat, attempting to sound a lot

spunkier than she felt. Now, she was sure it was Neil who had her at gun point. He both frightened and repulsed her, and she knew he was very volatile.

"Oh girlie, this can be gentle or I can be real rough, your choice." He slid his hand up to her breast, then withdrew it and chuckled. "Now, move, slow and easy, straight ahead. And don't get any ideas. I can wound you and still have fun," he sneered. Neil poked her in the back with the gun and she started moving slowly forward. She peered through the darkness, trying to see ahead as she walked. Suddenly there were shots behind them. Susanna jumped and gasped.

"Say goodbye to your sheriff," he chuckled. I know that gun. "Gary got him." He shoved her roughly and she stumbled forward. Tears stung her eyes at the thought of Jeff lying shot. She came to a trail and he poked her with the gun again. She kept walking, frantically looking for an opportunity to get away.

"Stop!" The man stood behind her, seeming to search the woods for the right direction. "Okay, git to the left along that log." They walked another hundred feet and then stepped onto a road. There was a car parked there. "Go to the car." She walked slowly, her knees shaking and her stomach churning.

If he got her in the car, he would take her somewhere and eventually, kill her. But, he had a gun. If she ran, he would shoot her. She had to think of something! Think, Susanna! Was there anything she could do?

He shoved her hard and she hit the side of the car. He shoved his pistol in his waistband and jerked her to face him, pressing himself hard against her.

"You feel good. We got time for one kiss before we get in the car, you know, a warm up for what is to come." He grabbed her face in his hands, but she twisted her face against his grip.

"No!" she cried. "Get off me!"

"You need to learn to cooperate," he sneered, drawing his open hand back. Susanna prepared herself for the blow. But instead, the man cried out in pain and was pulled away from her.

Jeff smashed his fist into the man's face, then brought up

his left in an uppercut to the stomach. Grabbing him by the jacket, he slammed his head into the car and the man slid to the ground. Jeff knelt with a knee in his back and brought his handcuffs off his belt and snapped them on the wrists of the unconscious man.

A light bar and headlights lit up the road and Bodie jumped out and ran towards Jeff.

"You got him, Sheriff?" The man on the ground was moaning now.

"Yeah, thanks Bodie, " said Jeff. "Take him, read him his rights, and get him to the station for booking."

"Sure thing, Sheriff." Bodie wrestled the stumbling man to the squad car and read him his rights before putting him in the back of the car.

Jeff turned to where Susanna stood trembling. He walked to her and took her by the arms, leaning down to look at her face. "Are you alright?" he asked. She shook her head up and down and started to sob. He moved his arms to pull her against his chest and let her cry. After several minutes, she pulled away and stepped back, wiping her eyes.

"What now?" she asked. In answer, he took her by one arm and led her over to another car that had pulled up. Marty got out and stood off to one side of the car.

"You sure you are okay?" he asked again.

"Yes, thank you!"

"Good," he said, opening the back door of the squad car. "Watch your head," he said as he firmly pushed her into the back seat.

"What…" she looked up at him in disbelief. "What are you doing? This is where you put the criminals!" He shut the door, leaving her there, as he locked the doors of the car. He spoke to Marty for a few minutes, then got in the front seat of the car and started to drive.

"Jeff!" she said through the metal mesh. "What are you doing? Let me out of here!" She was met with silence. "Jeff!" she snapped, banging her hand on the mesh. He ignored her. "I need to go get my car! Don't you dare do this to me again!"

"There is an extra set of handcuffs up here," he finally answered. "If you don't want to wear them, I suggest you sit back and be quiet." He spoke in a clipped, measured voice that made her catch her breath. His eyes met hers in the rear view mirror for a few seconds, and the coldness in them gave her chills. She sat back in the seat, stunned.

It was a long, quiet ride to the station. The air in the squad car bristled with tension. When they finally pulled into the parking lot, Susanna was glad, she wanted to be out of the car and away from Jeff right now. She just wanted to go home, take a shower and wash her hair. She imagined she could still smell that repulsive man on her.

He pulled up in front of the main door and parked the car. Without a word, he stepped out of the driver's seat and opened the back door of the squad car, extending his hand to help her out. His face was grim.

"Always the gentleman, huh?" She looked at his hand with distain, and stepped out of the car on her own. Defiance was plain on her face as she glared at him. She slammed the door.

"Thanks, Hop Along Cassidy! I'll call an Uber to get back to my car!" she snapped, turning to walk away. A strong hand grabbed her by the arm and placed her back against the side of the car. Her bravado faded as she caught a look at his face. His anger frightened her. He penned her in by putting his hands on either side of her on the car and leaning in so close she could feel his breath on her face.

"I told you to stay away from that mountain until we got those men in jail." His voice was low and he spoke slowly, between his teeth, like he was barely able to control himself. "I said you could get hurt. I pointed out that you could get my people hurt. But you went up there anyway."

"I have a job to do!" she protested. "I had to go!" She didn't even sound convincing to herself.

"So do I," he said, stopping after each word for emphasis. "My job is to keep you and my men alive!" He turned, and gripping her arm tightly, walked her into the office so fast she almost had to run to keep up. He held the door open and she thought about challenging him, but one look at his face choked the words in her throat.

He took her arm again when they got inside, and walked her over to a desk with a deputy sitting behind it in a stiff wooden chair. The deputy stood as the Sheriff approached him, his eyes moving back and forth between Jeff and Susanna. Jeff released her arm and pulled out a chair for her.

"Sit," he commanded, then turned to Stan. "Take her statement," Jeff said. "And when you are done," he glared at Susanna, "you keep her right here until I get back. " Jeff turned to walk away.

"But..." Susanna started, jumping to her feet. But she froze when Jeff whirled and fixed her with an icy stare. The silence hung like a fifty pound weight around her neck.

"Stan," he said, his eyes never leaving hers, "if she gives you any trouble, any at all, lock her in a cell until I get back."

"Yes Sir!" said Stan, looking at Susanna with renewed interest. Jeff turned and walked away. Stan cleared his throat. "Please sit down, M'am."

# Chapter 20

Susanna paced back and forth in front of Stan's desk. Stan did not seem to notice, even when she exhaled loudly. She stopped and stared at him once, but he never looked up from the report he was writing.

"It's been over three hours!" she said. Stan did not respond. She stared at him. Suddenly, she grabbed her purse. "That's it, I'm leaving!"

"I wouldn't do that, M'am." Stan said softly, without looking up.

"Why not? What are you going to do?"

"He will find you," said Stan as if it were a common occurrence. Susanna stared at him, her mouth open.

"Not if I don't want to be found!"

"He'll find you," Stan repeated. He continued writing his report as he spoke.

"Has anyone ever told you that you are exasperating?" she snapped.

"Yep! My wife tells me that all the time."

"Arrgh!" she yelled. Stan stood up.

"Gonna get coffee. Want some?"

"No! I just want the damn sheriff to come back!" she snarled.

"Looks like you're in luck," he said. Susanna followed his eyes and saw Jeff come through the outer door into the foyer. Jeff opened the inner door and stepped inside. He looked tired. He scanned the room until his eyes came to rest on hers. He locked eyes with her and walked slowly to the desk in front of her. He stood, and stared at Susanna. Reaching up, he took off his Stetson and glanced to the side as he started to set it on the desk.

"Where have you ..."she began, but stopped as his hand froze inches from the desk and he turned his eyes back on her again. He let the Stetson fall the few inches to the top of the desk, without breaking eye contact. His lips thinned to a grim line.

"This is ridiculous, I'm leaving!" She took a step forward,

but he did not move out of her way. Susanna felt her heart beat faster as he continued to hold her eyes, walking slowly towards her now, mouth set. He stopped five feet away and stared at her, hands on his hips. She felt the room closing in around her. She backed up the step she had taken and one more. Uncertain, she stood still.

"What the hell were you thinking?" He said it so quietly, she had to strain to hear him.

"I had to go; I have important work to do!" she spat, sudden anger making her voice rise.

"I told you not to go near that peak, it was dangerous." He spoke barely above a whisper.

"You can't tell me what to do!" she retorted. He hadn't moved.

"In this case, I can!" he growled. "Stop acting like a child; this isn't a game!"

"You have no authority over me!" Susanna said, sounding braver than she felt. His eyes flashed with a deep darkness she had never seen.

"If you ever disobey my orders again and put yourself or my people in danger, I will turn you over my knee and spank you!"

"You wouldn't dare!"

"You want to test that?" he said, eyes narrowed. He was taking slow, calculated steps toward her.

"You can't..." she stuttered, backing up against the wall. He took another step towards her. She couldn't breathe. He was only a foot away from her now; she could feel his body heat.

"I would be happy to show you I can," he said, reaching for her arm. She shrank back from his grip, riveted to his face, set in a coldness that made her knees feel shaky.

"Sheriff! You are a hard man to catch up to!" said Jeremy, bursting through the door. "Let me see that arm," said the EMT as he set down his bag. "Sit down, Sheriff." He looked back and forth between Susanna and Jeff. "Please," he said. Jeff tore his gaze away from Susanna and looked at Jeremy.

"It's just a scratch," he said. For the first time Susanna noticed the dark spot on the denim sleeve of his jacket, and the dark stains on the cuff of his shirt.

"You're hurt!" exclaimed, Susanna, the realization overtaking her as she saw the blood.

"Thanks to your stubborn refusal to listen!" he glared. Jeremy pushed him back on the desk and eased his jacket off. He slid Jeff's shirt off too, and Susanna gasped at the nasty laceration on his well muscled arm. Jeff grimaced as Jeremy started examining the wound on his arm.

"Is there anything I can do to help?" she asked. Jeremy glanced at her, then turned his attention back to Jeff's arm.

"Yeah, you can stay out of police business next time!" snapped Jeff.

"Thanks," said Jeremy, "I got this." He gave her a quick smile. "This is going to hurt, Jeff," said Jeremy. Jeff winced and nodded. He turned back to Susanna, but she was gone! The sound of the door shutting drew his eyes in time to see her glancing back at him before she hurried out of the station.

"Women!" Jeff growled. "Pain in my ass!" Jeremy smiled.

"Sheriff, do you want me to go get her?" asked Stan, rushing over to the desk.

"No," he said thoughtfully, shaking his head, "now that we have the men who were after her, she isn't in danger." He gave Stan a weak smile. "Besides, I might enjoy seeing her in a jail cell a little too much right now, and I need you here to keep things running smoothly until we all get back."

"Sure thing, Sheriff," said Stan.

"Jeremy, how much longer do you need? I have to get back out to the cabin and get that crime scene wrapped up."

"One more butterfly bandage, but you really need stitches." He shook his head, knowing Jeff wouldn't listen to him.

"First thing I'll do when the case is completed," said Jeff, putting his shirt back on and heading for the door. "Right now, we have bodies to find in the dark." Jeremy looked at Stan, who shrugged as the door closed behind Jeff.

"Didn't he say SHE was stubborn?" laughed Jeremy. Stan just grinned and sat down to work on his reports.

# Chapter 21

Susanna was shaking. She couldn't sort out her emotions. She was still frightened by being abducted, coming close to being killed, escaping, then being captured again. Then Jeff had rescued her. But, what did she feel about that? First, relief he had saved her from the repulsive Neil. Then shock, and then anger at being treated like a criminal.

"Who does he think he is, Raylon Givens?" she fumed to herself as she walked. But when he came back to the station, she saw something in him she had never seen. His simmering rage was so cold, so controlled, it made her feel even more unsettled.

She shook her head, trying to clear everything out of her mind. She wanted to just set all that had happened off to one side until she could analyze her feelings. Right now, she needed to get her car. She had practically run out of the station, worried for Jeff, and at the same time, afraid of what he might do. She walked along the street in the dark, pulling her phone out of her pocket. She quickly found the app on her phone and arranged for an Uber driver to pick her up in front of Allure Salon on Lake Tahoe Blvd. That wasn't too far to walk, and she thought it would help clear her head.

Susanna crossed the highway at Al Tahoe Blvd. and walked quickly to the small business complex. She only had a few minutes to wait before a silver Honda SUV pulled into the parking lot. The driver pulled up and rolled her window down.

"Are you Susanna?" asked the woman, her dark eyes sparkling. She immediately made Susanna feel comfortable.

"Yes," answered Susanna.

"I'm Dava," smiled the driver, "sit in the front or back, your choice. " Susanna opened the door and seated herself in the front passenger seat.

"You wanted to go out towards Kirkwood?" asked Dava. "Do you have a mileage point?"

"No, but if it is okay with you, I can direct you. My car is on the side of the road."

"I hate to ask, but I have seen it so many times…" began Dava, "you do have your keys with you, right?"

"Yes," Susanna laughed, "and I am sure you have had it happen more than once that a customer gets all the way out to their car without their keys! I can just guide you, thank you."

"Okay then, let's go," said Dava.

Susanna felt a prickly sensation run up her spine as she got out of Dava's car and prepared to get into her own. She rarely checked her car before she got in, but she took the time to do just that before she opened the door and got behind the wheel. She started her car, and waved a thank you to Dava as they both pulled back onto the road.

Susanna was exhausted. She could not wait to get home, take a hot shower, and slip under the covers of her own bed in her own home. Several minutes later, she pulled in the driveway and surveyed the front of her cabin. She still felt a little ill at ease, but she knew, in time, that she would again feel safe in her own home. She just had to chase away the nightmare of feelings that still flashed into her head sometimes.

Susanna put her key in the door and opened it to the smell of sage. She loved to put cut sage in a vase in her house; it was so soothing. She stepped into the living room, put down her pack, and then took a deep breath. Home. It felt good. She showered and was in bed in less than thirty minutes.

----

The eyes that watched her were not friendly. They watched long after she turned off the lights and went to bed. A seething anger was building and she would have to pay.

----

Susanna woke at dawn to a feeling of uncertainty. She

dressed quickly, then padded to the kitchen and made coffee. Sitting at her table, she gazed out the window at the forest. It always helped to be near the woods; nature could heal almost anything for her.

She tried to shake off the uneasy feeling she had. Was it concern over Jeff? Was she feeling the pressure to get back to work and accomplish what she came here to do? Was it just that it was over now and normal activity felt strange?

She decided she needed to work and restore some sense of normalcy to her life. Now that they caught the men last night, there was no danger. She would go back to the site of the shale slide to see if the Washoe remains were still there. It should be safe enough even for Jeff's paranoia at this point.

She rinsed out her coffee cup and checked her pack to make sure she still had the basic supplies. Taking one more look around the living area, she headed out the front door and got into her car. It felt good to be back on track!

---

The eyes watched her as she drove away. They followed her through the high powered binoculars and smiled with evil intent. He pulled his car out after her and followed at a good distance. There was no need to hurry; he knew where she was going. What he didn't know is that there was another pair of eyes following him.

# Chapter 22

Susanna turned down the road leading back towards the mountain. Her shoulders relaxed as she drove down the dirt road towards the area of the slide. She was back in her world, where she had a routine, a world where she could be by herself with nature, which she loved. She drove without hurry to the site of the slide, where she pulled her Subaru off the road, parking beside a boulder. The slide should be just on the other side, but she didn't want to drive too close and risk disturbing anything left.

She got out of her car, slinging her pack on her back. She began to walk around the base of the mountain until she reached the area she had slid down the talus. Carefully, she knelt and surveyed the rock debris at the base of the slope. She saw no sign of the skeletal remains that she had inadvertently unearthed as she slid down the mountain.

"Damn him!" she exclaimed, bitterness infused in her words. "I am so sorry," she said to the spirit of the Native American that had been desecrated. She felt responsible.

"You should be sorry," hissed a voice behind her. Susanna, leapt to her feet and whirled to face the voice. Her eyes widened and she felt sick to her stomach as she faced the man she knew as the Boss.

"You!" she cried. Her eyes were drawn to a large area of dried blood on his left shoulder. But that did not seem to hamper the grip he had on the Beretta, which was pointed straight at her stomach.

"In the flesh!" he said, a malicious grin spreading across his haggard face. "You ruined everything," he snarled, "all my men are dead and my business here is finished!"

"It should be! Your 'business' hurts others and destroys history," she retorted. "You have no decency, destroying graves and sacred ground for your own financial gain!" She knew it was dangerous to antagonize anyone with a gun pointed at her, but she didn't seem to be able to help herself.

"You just don't know when to shut up, do you?" He laughed, sending an ugly sound to her ears. "I just wish I could have let Neil give you what you deserve!" He took a silencer out of his pocket and screwed it into the threads on the end of the barrel of his gun. "Your boyfriend might have figured out they missed me and send someone out to nose around," he leered. "I wouldn't want anyone to hear the shots and come running too fast."

"Jeff could be near?" she asked in surprise. Her mind started to work. He might be looking for her if he realized the Boss wasn't with the others. If she could get to him, she would be safe! Desperately, her mind was searching for something she could do to fight him.

"Turn around and get moving!" he commanded, waving the gun impatiently.

"Why, so you can shoot me in the back?" Susanna was frantically trying to think of some way to defend herself so she could get away.

"Front or back makes no difference to me, in fact, I think I would enjoy seeing your face as you die! I just don't want to drag you any further than I have to." He grinned at her. "I want them to have to work to find your body."He took a step forward and shoved her.

Wildly, she looked around. What could she do? Her car was just on the other side of that boulder. If she could just get to it! She stopped and shook her head.

"I said move!" the Boss snarled, pushing her roughly. Susanna stumbled over a branch as he shoved her, and she fell to her knees. "Get up!" he yelled, kicking her hard in the leg.

"Ow!" she said, reflexively clutching the sand under her hand. She slipped her left hand into her pocket as she rose to a kneeling position. Securing her car keys in her left hand, she placed one foot on the ground and lifted herself slowly, then whirled quickly and threw a hand full of the sand in the face of the Boss. Then she ran as fast as she could.

A muffled shot sounded behind her and she was slammed

forward as burning pain shot through her right side. The force partially turned her, and she saw the Boss scratching at his eyes, while he swung the gun in her direction again. He was shooting blind! A little further! If only she could make it to the car. Another shot hit to her left just as she rounded the boulder. Quickly, she tore open the door of the car, praying she could get away before he caught up to her.

A strange zipping sound ripped the air. She couldn't place it, but she was getting in her car and focused on getting out of there. She started the car and shoved it into reverse, backing up a few feet before shifting into drive and accelerating quickly. She risked a glance in the rear view mirror, but all she saw was the cloud of dust she was creating. She had to get to Jeff. Mad or not, he would help her.

# Chapter 23

Jeff stood looking down at the men laid out on the ground in front of him as the sun crept higher over the mountains. Working in the dark was always difficult, but they had recovered three bodies and the evidence team was just wrapping up. A forest ranger and an off duty police officer were out with Tom, tracking down the fourth man. They found blood, but they had not found the body yet. He could be anywhere in the dense forest.

The woods around the cabin were pocked with bullet holes and the ground was churned by more than a dozen pair of boots running through here last night. With all the bullets flying in the dark, he was pleasantly surprised to find that he and a Highway Patrol officer, who had sprained an ankle dodging the gunfire, were the only ones injured on the side of the law.

His gaze returned to the deceased men on the ground. The young man bothered him the most. He couldn't be more than twenty-five or six, and now his life was ended. What a waste. He never got used to it, even when he knew he had no choice. He rubbed his eyes with the palms of his hands.

"Are they dead?" Susanna whispered.

"What in the hell are you doing here?" Jeff demanded, whirling towards her. He hadn't heard her come up to stand just behind him to one side. She just stood there, staring at the bodies. He felt a mixture of anger and despair; he knew she would never forget this sight as long as she lived. He wished there wasn't so much blood. "You're going home right now," he said, taking her by the arm and half dragging her to her car. As he reached the car, he spun her around to look at her.

"Jeff…" she started, looking up at him. Damn her, he could see the fear in her eyes and he hadn't wanted that. She should have listened to him and stayed away.

"Jeff, I needed to…"

"What you needed to do was listen to me!" He pulled her up hard against him, gripping her arms tight, and bringing his face inches from hers. "I don't even know what to do with you, Susanna! You won't listen to any reason, and now people are dead, and it could have been you, or me, or one of my officers! Part of me wants to throw you in a jail cell and let you sit for awhile, then charge you with obstruction of justice! But, I know that would seriously hurt your career, so I haven't done that to you! I threatened to spank you because the way you are acting is damn childish, and even that threat didn't stop you! I came close last night when you got me shot, and I swear, part of me still wants to turn you over my knee and dust your jeans but good!"

"Jeff, please…!" she cried, her eyes wide.

"Don't 'please Jeff' me, I have had it with you, and I suggest you get out of my sight right now before I do something I'm not sure I want to do! Now go home!" he snapped. He yanked the door to her car open and pushed her carefully but firmly inside, then shut the door. He turned and strode back to the group of men standing by the bodies. He was angry – at her, at himself, at the whole situation. What was he going to do with her? Damn it!

"Coroner's wagon is on the way," said Stan. He sighed. "Shame she had to see this," he said, glancing towards Susanna's car.

"It's her own damn fault!" Jeff snapped. "I told her to stay away." He rubbed his hands over his tired face. "I have never met a woman so stubborn! This isn't a game!" The deputies stood silent for a minute, looking at the dead men and waiting for the coroner.

"You sure you didn't get a little carried away with that confrontation?" asked Marty quietly. He was looking at her car. "She hasn't moved since you put her in the car."

Jeff looked back over his shoulder in the direction of her car. Why was she still here? He told her to go home; why couldn't she just listen to him on this?

"How the hell did you get so much blood on your pants? You hit?" asked Bodie, walking up from the gully. They all followed his eyes to the thigh of Jeff's pant leg. The blood was fresh.

"What?" he said, looking down at his pant leg, "I'm fine, I..." he said. He stared at Bodie for a few seconds, then turned to look at the car, realization dawning. Susanna was slumped against the wheel. "Jeremy, follow!" he shouted as he ran to her car. "Susanna!" he yelled.

She did not move. He ripped open the car door and reached in to sit her up. She moaned as his arm went around her waist. He felt the warm, wet spot on his arm and saw the red as he sat her up. "Susanna, stay with me!" he pleaded as he looked at the paleness of her face.

"Help me get her out of the car," said Jeremy behind him. Jeff moved against the door and Jeremy shifted around to the other side of the seat so they could lift her out with support on both sides. Gently, they lowered her to the ground and Jeremy took her vitals. Jeff stared at the large, dark spot on her black top, lifting it carefully.

"Looks like a through and through," said Jeremy," but we need to get her to the hospital." He looked at Jeff. "She's lost a lot of blood."

The sound of the approaching ambulance was a welcome one. Jeff helped lift her onto the gurney, and watched as Jeremy secured the IV. Carefully, they lifted the gurney into the back of the ambulance. As the driver shut the doors, Jeff turned and ran to his car.

Both vehicles ran hot, full out, with light bars and sirens and made the twenty-five miles to the hospital in record time. Jeff pulled up right behind the ambulance and jumped out as the waiting medical staff hoisted the gurney out of the back of the ambulance.

"Type her and get her prepped for surgery," said an emergency room doctor to a nurse, as they wheeled the gurney rapidly through the corridor reserved for ambulance admissions. "What's her name?" he asked.

"Susanna," answered the EMT.

"Susanna, this is Dr, Josephy," he said to the unconscious

woman. "I'm not going to let go of you, so hang on for me!"

Jeff ran into the corridor just in time to hear the doctor and see them wheeling her into an elevator, while a nurse walked rapidly down the hall towards a man in a lab coat, coming to meet her. The man took the vial of blood from her and walked rapidly away. He felt slightly relieved, hearing the firm tone in the doctor's voice. He too believed unconscious people could hear you, and he was glad the doctor had reassured Susanna.

---

Two hours later, Jeff was sitting next to her bed in recovery, watching her breathe. Her face was so pale.

"How's she doing?" asked Jeremy, coming into the room.

"She hasn't come out of the anesthesia yet," answered Jeff. Doctor Josephy said they stopped the bleeding, cleaned it up and gave her a few stitches, but she should be okay. He is still concerned about the loss of blood." He sighed. "I can't believe I didn't notice she had been shot," said Jeff.

"Don't be so hard on yourself," said Jeremy, "you were busy recovering from a gunshot wound yourself, and wrapping up the investigation." He studied Jeff. "Besides, she was wearing all black – hard to see blood on black clothes."

Jeff sat by her bed, watching her sleep. So many questions were running through his head. How did she get shot? She wasn't hurt when he put her in the car to go back to the station. It had to happen when she ran out of the station while Jeremy was working on him.

"She went to get her car!" he exclaimed, realization dawning. She had her car back when she showed up beside him near the men who had been shot. " How did she get out to her car?" He looked at Jeremy, knowing he didn't have the answer.

"I don't know," said Jeremy, "I followed you back out here after you left the station. I didn't see her."

"Uh, boss?" said Bodie. Jeff had not heard him come into the room. "How is she?" he asked, gesturing toward Susanna, who still lay unconscious.

"The doctor says she will be alright," he answered. He rubbed his hands over his face and wished he had a good cup of coffee.

"That's a relief," said Bodie, and meant it. He ran a hand through his hair.

"Yeah, Bodie," said Jeff, while both men stared in silence at the woman in the bed for a few more minutes.

"Is everything wrapped up?" asked Jeff, turning back to Bodie.

"Well, not exactly," began Bodie, twisting his hat through his hands.

"Just tell me," said Jeff, bristling with tension now.

"Tom came back with the other two officers." He took a deep breath. "We only found three bodies, Sir." He was miserable as he looked at Jeff. "It looks like the Boss is still on the loose." Jeff stared at him in disbelief. That meant Susanna was still in danger!

"I want a guard on her twenty-four hours a day," he said, looking at Bodie. "Six hour shifts so nobody gets too tired and lets their guard down."

"Yes Sir." Bodie shifted from one foot to the other and looked down at his hat.

"It's not your fault, Bodie," said Jeff softly.

"Thanks, Sheriff," said Bodie. "I just feel so bad about the whole thing."

"I know, Bodie," said Jeff. "That's what makes you such a good lawman." Bodie's head jerked up like he wasn't sure he heard right. Jeff smiled at him and Bodie smiled back, blushing a little.

"And I know what you are thinking. We are short handed and everyone is tired," Jeff continued. Bodie nodded. "Call Chris and see if she would like to extend her contract work to include some watch duty. She's good, and Susanna knows her." Jeff thought for a moment. "Why don't you give Tom a call as well. Maybe he would take some off duty extra work."

"Good ideas, Sheriff. I'll get right on it." He turned to

leave, but Jeff stopped him.

"Bodie?"

"Yes?" He looked at Jeff with expectation, waiting for further orders.

"Schedule yourself off for a day and get some sleep." Jeff smiled at his top deputy.

"I'm fine, Sir, I…"he protested.

"Bodie, that's an order." At Bodie's stricken look, he added "I can't have my best deputy worn to a frazzle. Who would back me up?" Bodie's face actually turned a bright red now, and he looked down at his shoes.

"Yes, Sir. Thank you Sir," he said, looking at Jeff with brighter eyes and smiling shyly. Jeff could swear he walked a little taller as he left the room.

# Chapter 24

Susanna was moved to her own room as soon as her vitals were stable. She had opened her eyes briefly, but closed them before she said anything. Jeff was still sitting by Susanna's bed when Chris showed up at midnight.

"How is she?" Chris inquired.

"Still out of it. The doctor said she will be alright, but she has lost a lot of blood." Chris studied him silently for a few minutes, then pulled a chair over and sat down next to him.

"Talk," she said simply, staring him in the eyes. She leaned back in her chair with her legs and arms crossed.

"About what?" he asked.

"Don't pull that on me, cowboy, I know you too well. What's eating you up?"

Jeff resisted for a few minutes, squirming in his chair. Then he gave up. He relayed the events of the past twenty-four hours while Chris sat impassively and listened. She nodded once or twice, but otherwise, just let him spill it all. When he finished, he sat forward, his elbows on his knees, and rubbed his face.

"I should have..."

"Stop it."

"What?"

"Stop that. You know better than to shoulda coulda woulda yourself. You did the best you could." She leaned forward and put a hand on his shoulder. "This was tough. She wouldn't listen, she is a determined woman. And those were some really bad guys."

"Remember, one is still missing."

"We'll get him. You have done almost everything right to protect her and catch them."

"Almost?" he said with surprise. "What did I miss?" She looked pointedly at the bed next to Susanna.

"Sleep," she said, with a look that said she would tolerate no nonsense.

"I'm fine!"

"No, you aren't," she insisted. "When is the last time you slept?"

"Just," he started, then stopped to think. "Two days ago, but I'm fine!"

"Look, you aren't going to think clearly or do anyone any good if you don't get some sleep. Take advantage of me being here and sleep while I watch. You'll be right here when she wakes up."

"Okay," he agreed grudgingly, "but make sure you wake me when your shift is over."

"What shift?" she grinned.

"I don't understand, didn't Bodie call you?"

"Yes. I am scheduled for tomorrow night. This one is for an old friend." She smiled again. "Now, get your butt in bed…but keep your pants on," she laughed.

"Anybody ever tell you that you have a mean streak?" he chided as he walked over to the bed. He took off his boots, took off his jacket, pulled his shirt out of his jeans, and sat down on the bed. He took off his holster and lay his gun on the bed next to him. He stretched out on the bed and was asleep before Chris replied.

"Yep," she said to the sleeping form. "Mean is what it takes sometimes." She stood and checked Susanna again, then slid her chair over between Susanna's bed and the door. She left the blinds open so she could see anyone approaching the room. She reached inside her jacket and withdrew her gun, checked the magazine again, and settled the gun in her lap, under a brochure she took off the table on the side of the room. No one was coming into that room to hurt Susanna or Jeff, as long as she was drawing breath.

---

Jeff's eyes shot open as dawn was breaking over the mountains. He sat up in bed, looking around, momentarily forgetting where he was. Chris smiled at him and went back to watching the door. Jeff looked at Susanna. She was still sleeping.

He took a minute to go into the bathroom and splash some water on his face. He looked in the mirror at the drawn face staring back at him. He rubbed his hand over the dark stubble of beard that had appeared in the past couple of days. He came out of the bathroom just as the doctor came into the room.

The doctor walked to the bed and listened to Susanna's heart. When he began to remove the bandage to check the wound, she stirred and opened her eyes.

"What happened?" she asked, confused. "Where am I? Who are you?" she said to the doctor.

"You are in the hospital," Dr. Josephy replied, "you have been shot." Her eyes widened and she looked at Jeff, who was now standing beside the bed, watching her.

"Did you get him?" she asked, breathing rapidly.

"Who? Did you see who shot you?" asked Jeff, leaning in closer.

"The Boss guy! He shot me! I went out to the slide area where the Washoe grave was, and he followed me!" Jeff's eyes blazed.

"You went where?" he asked in a low, clipped voice.

"Out to where I slid down the talus slope, where they caught me! He was there!" Jeff looked at her in astonishment, then turned and walked to the other side of the room.

"Looks like you are healing well," the doctor said, looking from one to the other. "Just stay in bed and don't get too excited. You need to rest."

"I could handcuff her to the bed to make sure she listens to you," Jeff said, turning back around, his mouth set in an angry line.

"I don't think that will be necessary," said the doctor, starting to laugh. The laugh died in his throat as he looked at Jeff's face.

"I don't think you know your patient as well as I do, doc," said Jeff, glaring at Susanna. What in the hell was the matter with her? "I think she either thinks she is immortal or has a death wish," he said with conviction.

"Who do you…" she started.

"Think I am?" he finished for her. " I'm the Sheriff, and I warned you!" Suddenly, Bodie walked into the room.

"Can I talk to you outside, Sheriff?" he asked.

"Sure," he replied, hearing the urgency in Bodie's voice. He pulled his eyes off Susanna and followed the deputy into the hall.

---

"We went out to the shale slide like you thought we should," he said, "and we found a lot of blood."

"Go ahead," prompted Jeff.

"But we haven't found the body yet." Bodie looked worried. "There was so much blood, we couldn't figure out how whoever was shot could still be alive. But we looked all over and found nothing but a car, about a mile from all the blood."

"Anything in the car?" asked Jeff.

"No registration, just a lot of blood on the driver's seat. But the blood on the seat was dry and the blood near the slide was fresh." Bodie shook his head. "The team is still going over the car." He glanced at Susanna. "Is she doing better?"

"That depends on how you look at it," said Jeff. Then noting Bodie's confused look, he added, "Medically, she is better."

"Ah!" said Bodie, getting the drift. She and Jeff were still butting heads. "I will let you know if we find anything when the team is done."

"Okay, Bodie, we'll keep the guard here until we find the body. Keep me posted."

"Sure thing, Sheriff," said Bodie as he turned to walk back down the corridor.

Jeff smiled as he watched him leave. He had a pretty good

idea what had happened.

---

Jeff walked back in the room as the doctor was leaving.

"She needs rest," he said pointedly to Jeff.

"I wish she knew that," retorted Jeff. Chris stood up as he came back in the room.

"I think I am going to head out and get some sleep myself before my shift tonight," she said. She raised her eyebrows as she looked at Jeff. "Good luck," she whispered.

Jeff shut the door behind her and looked at Susanna. She was sitting up in bed, but she was not looking at him. Her eyes were downcast and she was twisting the cover on the bed between her fingers. His heart softened as he looked at her. Damn it! Why couldn't he just stay mad at her!

He walked over and sat on the bed beside her. She still didn't look at him. He cupped her chin in his hand and raised her head, but her eyes were still lowered.

"Susanna," he said simply. It surprised him how well he could read her after knowing her only a few days. Her chin began to quiver and suddenly she burst into tears. He took her in his arms and stroked her hair as she sobbed on his chest.

"I was so scared!" she cried, her voice catching between the words.

"It's alright now," he said. "You're safe here." He moved his hand gently between her shoulder blades, afraid to rock her as she continued to cry. He didn't know how much pain she was feeling and was concerned about moving her too much and disturbing the wound.

"Jeff?" she asked, as her sobs subsided.

"Yes, Susanna," he replied.

"I really am sorry," she said in a small voice. She was clutching the back of his shirt in her fists like she was afraid he would leave and she needed to hold him here. She was shaking.

He stroked her hair for a few more minutes, then carefully pulled back and looked at her.

"I just couldn't stand the thought of you getting hurt," he said. They stared into each other's eyes for several minutes, before Susanna looked down at the blanket. "Are you in a lot of pain?" he asked.

"No, not really," she answered.

"Good," he said. "I think there is still a lot of medication in your system," he said. She nodded and looked at him.

"How is your arm?" she asked, remembering he had been shot the night before.

"I'm fine," he said, "I've had worse." His face clouded. "Susanna..." he hesitated.

"What?" she asked, reading his concern.

"We haven't caught the Boss yet," he said, watching her eyes widen. "But, I have officers who will be here twenty-four seven, so you will be safe."

"I...I..." she was starting to breathe rapidly.

"Susanna!" he said firmly, to bring her eyes back to his. "You are safe; it is okay now." He watched her face relax. "Besides," he said, "I have a feeling we will catch him very soon."

"I'm tired now, "she said suddenly, her eyes closing. She seemed to actually wilt in his arms. Gently, he lowered her back on the bed and pulled the blanket over her chest.

He looked up as Tom opened the door, and seeing Susanna starting to doze, motioned for him to step into the hall. Jeff and Tom talked in whispers for several minutes, and then Tom left again. Jeff was smiling when Marty walked up to relieve him. He held a travel mug of coffee and the aroma wafted in Jeff's direction. He realized he hadn't eaten in more than twenty-four hours and needed fresh clothes.

"Did you get any sleep Marty?" asked Jeff.

"Yes Sir," he said, "I got a solid six hours and am good to go." Jeff nodded.

"Did you eat?" he asked.

"Yes, sir, my wife had breakfast for me when I got up."

"She's asleep again, so I think I am going to run home and shower. "I'll be back in a couple hours."

"Copy that," said Marty, settling down to watch the door.

Chapter 25

The shower, shave, and fresh clothes made Jeff feel like a new man. The three hours sleep didn't hurt either. He made a few phone calls, then filled a travel mug with good, fresh coffee, and headed off to the hospital. His first stop was not Susanna's room, though.

"A promise is a promise, doc, and I promised our department EMT that I would get this stitched up as soon as I closed the case." said Jeff.

"The butterflys have done a decent job of holding it together, but I am afraid it needs to be cleaned out again before I stitch you up, "said Doctor Josephy. "I won't ask what you have been doing since you got shot, but it wasn't a sterile environment." He peeled off the bandages and began to clean the wound.

"How many stitches?" asked Jeff, admitting to himself it stung.

"I'd say five or six will do it," he said, but I am going to give you a shot of antibiotics too, just to be safe." He started stitching the wound. "You say you closed the case? You found the man that shot that young woman?"

"I'd say we are close enough," said Jeff.

"That's good to hear," he said. "Try to keep this clean, and come back in three days to get the stitches removed and check for infection." He turned to the tray beside him, picked up a syringe, and smiled. Jeff stood, turned around, and dropped his jeans.

---

The phone on his hip buzzed as Jeff walked into Susanna's room. She was awake, so he took it in the room.

"Sheriff, I am out a few miles beyond Sorenson's Resort right now, and we have something really interesting here," said Bodie.

"Go ahead," said Jeff.

"We got a call about a dead body propped against a rock in a guy's yard."

"Do you have an ID on the body?" he asked.

"I think we just found the Boss," said Bodie. Jeff straightened, looked at Susanna's inquiring face, and stepped outside the door.

"How sure are you of the ID?"

"Well, he looks something like the sketch Susanna did with Don, but ..." he trailed off. "Before we release it to the press, I am sure you are going to want the coroner to do an autopsy and our lab to run some tests."

"Cause of death?" asked Jeff.

"Looks like a rifle shot to the head, which is why I can't be more positive on the ID."

"Just one shot?" asked Jeff.

"Yeah, hell of a shot, too. I would have thought if Tom got him, he would let us know." Bodie blew out a breath on the other end of the line. "He also has an older wound in his left shoulder, but it is the head shot that killed him."

"Who called it in?" asked Jeff.

"That's where it gets even more interesting," said Bodie. "The home owner called it in. Jeff, the body is propped up against a boulder with a petroglyph on it, sitting right in his front yard."

"What?" Jeff was not expecting that. "Do we have proof it is genuine?"

"Even better, " said Bodie, "the homeowners were so spooked by finding a dead man against the boulder in their front yard, they figure it is some kind of jinx or a sign the spirits of the Washoe are coming for them. They are with Stan right now, giving a statement about how they bought it from a guy who had a couple of his men deliver it."

"That is even better than we hoped!" exclaimed Jeff.

"We're going to take them in and show them shots of the two younger men we have on file and see if they can connect them to the purchase."

"This is excellent work, Bodie, keep me posted."

"Copy that," said Bodie, and disconnected the call.

Jeff turned to see Susanna watching him anxiously. But, he took time to make a call before he went in to tell her the news. He walked back into the room and Marty stood, waiting expectantly.

"We haven't officially verified it yet, but we are pretty sure we just found the Boss," said Jeff. Susanna gasped and put her hands to her face.

"Is he…" she whispered.

"Yes," said Jeff, "he is dead." He walked over to Marty and clapped him on the shoulder. "Thanks, Marty, I'll stick around here. Why don't you go back to the station or take a break?"

"Thanks, Sheriff, I'll head back to the station and see what I can do there to help." Marty left with a smile on his face. It felt good when it came together.

Jeff pulled a chair over to the bed and sat down. Susanna looked at him, her mouth slightly open, but she did not say a word. Her face was pale, and her hands were shaking. He leaned forward and took her hands in his.

"It's normal to feel a sense of shock when it's over," he said. "Bodie will be here soon to confirm, and then you can really relax."

"Thank you," she nodded.

"Oh good, you are awake," said the nurse's aide as she carried a tray into the room. She set it on the side table, and wheeled it over to the bed, placing it over Susanna's lap. "Our kitchen is very good here," said the perky blond, removing the plate cover to reveal chicken, rice, and carrots. "The doctor would like to see you eat something."

"I am hungry," said Susanna, with surprise. "I think it has been more than a day since I ate!" The aide smiled.

"Sheriff, can I get you a plate?" asked the young woman. "It's no trouble, and no charge," she bubbled.

"Are you sure?" His stomach had started to rumble as he realized he hadn't eaten much in the past twenty-four hours either.

"Positive! Chicken okay?" He looked at Susanna's plate

again and nodded.

"That would be great, thank you!" She returned in a few minutes with another plate for Jeff, and wheeled the other tray in the room over to him. He and Susanna were eating in companionable silence when she returned a few minutes later and gave them each an ice cream cup.

"Enjoy!" she said and gave them a wink. They looked at each other and shared a laugh.

"I think she has enough energy for both of us," said Susanna.

"That's the truth," laughed Jeff, as they ate their ice cream.

## Chapter 26

Jeff and Susanna had just finished the meal when the aide came back to collect the dishes. Jeff caught her name on her badge.

"Thank you, Cheryl, you were right! The kitchen does a great job!"

"I'll tell them you said so," she beamed. She was nearly to the door with the dishes when Bodie walked in.

"Oh, excuse me M'am," he said, stepping out of her way and removing his hat. "Do you need some help with those?"

"Why, thank you, deputy, how sweet!" Cheryl said, bestowing a big smile on him. "I'm fine, but can I get you something to eat?"

"Oh, I wouldn't want you to go to any trouble, M'am," said Bodie.

"It's no trouble at all, and from what I hear around the hospital, you guys have been working all night catching the bad guys."

"Well, yes M'am, that's true," said Bodie, shifting from foot to foot and smiling sheepishly.

"You have a seat then, and I'll be back with a plate for you too," she purred, winking at him. Bodie's eyes followed her out the door.

"Bodie?" asked Jeff, grinning.

"Yes Sir?" he said, still looking out the door.

"Did you have something to tell me," smirked Jeff, tamping down a chuckle.

"Oh. Yes, yes I did," he said, coming back into focus. He looked at Susanna, then at Jeff.

"At this stage of the game, I think she can hear it all," said Jeff, answering Bodie's unspoken question.

"Okay," he exhaled with relief, then brought a chair closer to the bed. Cheryl returned with a plate for Bodie.

"Here ya go, deputy," she smiled, as she pulled the tray over and set the plate in front of him. She took a carton of milk out of her pocket and set it down on the tray.

"Thank you, M'am," he said without even looking at the plate, "that's awful nice of you."

"You need anything else, you know where to find me, Sugar." Cheryl winked at Bodie and breezed out of the room, with his eyes watching every step she took. Susanna giggled and Jeff laughed, bringing Bodie's head back around. He blushed bright red when he realized what they were laughing about.

"It's okay, Bodie, she is very cute and exceptionally nice," said Jeff.

"Yes," he said, clearing his throat. He sat up straighter as he took a bite of food. "Sorry, he apologized, I haven't eaten since yesterday."

"I think we're all in that boat," said Tom, walking in with a bag in his hand. He grabbed another chair and dug a sandwich and a Coke out of the bag. "This a briefing?" He took a bite of his sandwich and looked at Jeff and Bodie.

"Why don't I fill you in on what Bodie found this morning, and then he can finish when he is done eating?" Jeff glanced at Bodie, who nodded approval while he put another fork full of rice in his mouth.

Jeff brought Tom up to speed while the two men ate. Susanna listened alternately with fascination and horror showing on her face. Tom listened without comment, finishing his sandwich with a raised eyebrow or two along the way. When Jeff finished, he looked at Bodie, who was just wiping his hands.

"The latest since this morning is that the dead man has definitely been identified as a wanted felon, well known for dealing in the illegal sale of antiquities and Native American artifacts," said Bodie. Using fingerprints, we were able to make a positive ID."

"You're sure it's the Boss?" whispered Susanna, her face pale.

"Yes M'am, " said Bodie gently. "Real name Otto Suss. Suspect in several unsolved murders as well. AKA, the Boss."

Susanna deflated like a balloon when a child lets go of the

neck and the air whooshes out. She fell back on the pillow with both hands covering her eyes as she wept. The three men sat silently, not quite knowing what to do, but understanding she was crying with pent up relief. After several minutes, she wiped her eyes and looked at them sheepishly. Jeff handed her the handkerchief out of his breast pocket and she wiped her face and nose.

"I don't know why I am crying now," she said. "I never cry, and lately it seems I cry all the time!"

"It's normal," said Jeff, "don't think twice about it." He squeezed her hand gently. "It's the let down when a tense situation is finally resolved."

"That was one heck of a shot," said Bodie, changing the subject by speaking to Tom.

"What are you talking about?" asked Tom, a puzzled look on his face.

"The Boss! Taking him out with a single rifle shot to the head is a tough shot. Most people wouldn't risk a miss, they would go for the body mass."

"You think I shot the guy you found in Hope Valley?" asked Tom.

"Well, yeah, " said Bodie, confused. Tom was shaking his head back and forth.

"I didn't shoot him."

"Then who shot him?" asked Bodie, looking at Jeff in total bewilderment.

"I did," said a voice from the door way. All eyes turned to the tall man in fatigues standing in the doorway. Susanna gasped.

"Who are you?" asked Bodie, standing.

"Sam!" Susanna clasped her hands together and held them against her lips. "Oh, I can't believe it's you!" Tears were streaming down her face as Sam walked to the bed. He sat on the edge of the bed and leaned forward to hug her. He held her gently for a few minutes, then pulled back.

"It's good to see you, Sis, even under these circumstances," said Sam.

"How did you get here?" she asked, beaming.

Sam winked at her, then stood and smiled at Jeff. He walked over and extended his hand. The two men smiled at each other as they shook hands.

"You must be Jeff," said Sam. Then he turned and extended a hand to Tom. "And you are Tom," he said with assertion, as they shook hands. "Didn't see much of you, but when I did, I recognized another Special Forces man." Tom smiled and nodded.

"Thought I felt eyes on me a time or two," he said, "and I caught a glimpse of movement once." Sam grinned and turned back to Jeff.

"Glad you could make it," said Jeff. "As soon as Bodie told me it was a rifle shot, I had a feeling it was you."

"Wait a minute, how do you two know each other?" asked Susanna from her bed.

"Jeff called the Smithsonian when the trouble first started," said Sam. "With the help of Tom Wilcox here, and your boss, Rebecca, they navigated the government contacts until they got a message to me that you were in trouble." He smiled at Susanna as her mouth gaped open. "It wasn't too difficult to get leave, since I hadn't been stateside in over two years."

"Why didn't you tell me you were coming?" Susanna demanded.

"That was my idea," said Jeff. "Until we caught all the bad guys, I thought it would be good to have an ex Army Ranger and a top notch Marine rifle expert out there that nobody knew about."

"I can't believe you kept it from me!" she fumed.

"Little sister," said Sam, "you always had a stubborn streak. From what I hear, you weren't listening to Jeff and he had his hands full keeping you out of trouble." He grinned. "I think he is a right smart man to ask for help with you." He winked at Jeff, then leaned over his sister. "I have to say though, I think you finally met your match!"he said in a loud whisper. Laughter lit up the room.

"I have to admit," Sam said, soberly. "When I saw that man shoot you, it nearly made me crazy," he said, stroking Susanna's cheek.

"You were there?" she gasped.

"Yeah, up the hill a bit. I watched him last night as he was watching your house."

"He was watching me last night?" she exclaimed. "I had the weirdest feeling someone was watching me!"

"We both were," smiled Sam. "But neither of you knew I was watching. I followed him this morning when he followed you. I was set up to take him when you threw the sand in his face." He grinned. "Good thinking, by the way. But you jumped up and ran right at me. You were between him and me. I couldn't shoot him without risking hitting you," he looked at her sadly.

"Oh Sam!" she winced.

"I scrambled a little and got a better bead just as you started around the boulder and he started shooting again. I got him as you went around the rock." His eyes were deep and sad.

"No wonder he didn't follow me," she mused.

"But neither could I," he said sadly." I could stop the threat, but I couldn't get to you before you drove away." He touched her cheek. "I knew you were hurt, and I couldn't help you."

"Oh, Sam, I didn't know!" He nodded.

"Sound carries out there and I heard you say Jeff might be near. I was hoping you would go to him," he said, looking at Jeff.

"She did." He looked at the floor. "And I blew it." Jeff sent an apologetic look to first Sam, then Susanna. They had trusted him, and he did not handle it well.

"You got her here, didn't you?" asked Sam with open appreciation.

"Yes, he did," spoke Susanna, soft eyes meeting Jeff's. "And he got you here, too," she said, taking Sam's hand in hers.

"How did you get him to Hope Valley and how did you know about that petroglyph?" asked Bodie.

"I could tell you, but…" Sam said and he and Tom

laughed. "I had a tarp in my vehicle and I wrapped him up."

"I had a report that some people had a boulder with a petroglyph on it in their front yard," said Tom. "I confirmed it just before you called me in to help, but I didn't have time to prove anything. When Sam called to say he had the target, we decided to see if we could help the justice system along a little bit." His eyes sparkled.

"I'd say a little guilt and a dead body worked pretty well," interjected Jeff.

"Well, I'll be damned!" said Bodie.

"Oh, I have something for you, Susanna," said Sam, walking back over to the bed. He reached in his pocket and brought out a small pink rock with red stripes and held it out to her.

"My rock!" she cried. "Sam, where did you...?" she asked, looking at him with surprise.

"I uh, checked his pockets before we set him against the boulder." He leaned over and kissed her on the top of the head.

"Sam, thank you. I get to see you and you gave me back a special memory." Her eyes shone as she and her brother exchanged a long overdue look of sibling love. Finally, the men stood up and everyone shook hands again.

"I'm going to let you catch up with your sister," said Tom." It's been a real pleasure."

"Thanks for all your help in this case,"said Bodie.

"I am very grateful for your assistance," said Jeff, "and definitely your help in keeping your sister alive!" Both men looked at Susanna, who took her turn at adding color to her cheeks.

"I'll see you all before I leave, "said Sam.

"Lookin' forward to it," said Tom. "I'll take this watch," said Sam to Jeff, who grinned as he left with the others.

## Chapter 27

Jeff stood looking at the long table with everything they had taken from the Boss' car. He hadn't seen Susanna in the three days since she left the hospital, and he guessed that was fine with her because she hadn't called. Well that's the way it is when a case is over, he thought. Maybe she wanted to be rid of him. He was keeping himself busy, trying to remind himself she was a pain in the ass and he had work to do.

They had found a small ledger book belonging to Otto Suss inside one of the door panels, with names and contact information for buyers. There were a few pictures tucked in the book as well, and they were hoping to match those to some of the stolen artifacts in the national data base. They turned both of those over to the FBI, since it involved several states.

There was a pneumatic drill, some rock picks, a few brushes, and a headlamp. The lab techs had found minute particles of rock and dirt on the tools, and were working to match the samples to areas of known theft.

They found a small bag of amphetamine and a flask of whiskey. That fit with Susanna's view that the Boss looked older than he was because he drank heavily and, apparently, also used some serious drugs.

They also found a lap top, although it had been smashed. The tech team had been able to get some information off the hard drive; enough to see the computer was Susanna's. He blew out a breath.

"I guess I should tell her we have it, and can give her copies of what we were able to retrieve," he said to the empty room.

His gaze continued down the table to the pile of trash they had found in the trunk. Idly, Jeff looked at a crumpled brown bag with a liquor store logo on it. It had been stuffed in the side pocket in the trunk area, with some flares and a few smaller pieces of trash. He scanned the table again, feeling like he was missing something. He picked through the trash, not sure what he was looking for. His gloved hand spread the trash apart, looking for more evidence. He picked up a small, smashed McDonald's bag and opened it, just in case. A small velvet cloth bag fell out of the fast food bag onto the table. Carefully, Jeff picked up the cloth bag and opened it. This, he could use. He would go talk to the District Attorney right now.

———————————

   Sam and Susanna were sitting in chairs on her tiny deck area outside the back door. The forest was peaceful and they were sharing memories of growing up, and talking about the future.
   "I have one more tour, and then I think I will hang up my boots and come back here," said Sam. I miss the clear air and the calm majesty of the mountains."
   "It's where we learned what life was supposed to be," she said. "Now that I have work near here, I will be able to stay at home more. I am going to request assignments on the West coast in the future."
   "I'm sorry about the arrowheads," said Sam. I know how important they were to you."
   "Yeah. Well, what's that saying about they can't take the memories?" She laughed, but Sam knew there was pain underneath. "At least you brought me the rock back, and I have the picture."She smiled affectionately at Sam.
   "How are you feeling?" he asked.
   "Really good, actually," she said. "The doctor said since I was in good shape, and young, I am healing faster than expected."
   "How's the pain?"
   "I really don't have much, unless I move too fast or reach for something high. Then it pulls a little." She shook her head. "But, you know how our family is – we have a high tolerance for pain, so I still have most of the pain meds left." They both laughed.

"Have you seen Jeff?" he asked, watching her reaction.

"No," she said, avoiding his eyes. "He hasn't come around since the hospital. I think he is glad to get rid of me." She was twisting her hands again.

"He's a good man, little sister. I'd feel much better going back if I knew someone like him was watching out for you."

"I can take care of myself!" she protested.

"How's that working for you?" he said, fixing her with a stare that said otherwise. She brought her head up in surprise. He held up a hand before she could speak. "I know you are smart, capable, strong, and all that. But I would worry less if I knew someone with some savvy was looking for you to come home and would go find you if you didn't."

"Yeah, well, I don't think it will be Jeff. I think I am too independent for his tastes."

"Independent?" he raised an eyebrow. "Try stubborn beyond reason sometimes! But still, I saw more than him just doing his job." His eyes shot to the corner of the house so quickly, Susanna turned.

"Am I interrupting?" asked Jeff, walking towards them.

"Not at all," said Sam. "We were just wondering how you were doing," grinned Sam, shooting his sister a look of satisfaction. She turned her back slightly to Jeff and stuck her tongue out at her brother.

"I have some information about your computer," said Jeff, standing uneasily as he looked at Susanna.

"Oh, did you find it?" she asked hopefully.

"Yes, but I am afraid it is ruined." Her face fell. "We were able to get some information off the hard drive, though," he said, extending his hand with two thumb drives. "Since it is all about your work and nothing to do with the case, the District Attorney gave me permission to give these to you."

"Thank you," she said quietly, as she accepted the thumb drives. She studied his face. "I guess I will have to get a new lap top, but I am very grateful that you were able to retrieve at least some of my work." She smiled and saw his face relax.

"That's good news, Jeff, " said Sam. "And it was very nice of you to bring them all the way out here." He looked at his sister.

"It's my pleasure," he said, shifting his eyes from Sam back to Susanna. He cleared his throat. "I thought you might like these back too," said Jeff. He held her eyes as he reached in his pocket and came out with a small cloth bag, which he extended to her.

Her heart caught in her throat as she rose and tore her eyes away from his face to look at the small package in his palm. She reached for the bag with a trembling hand, then raised her eyes to his as she closed her hand over the bag. She opened it slowly and couldn't believe her eyes!

"Are these?" she said, her eyes huge in her face. Her lips were parted in wonder.

"Yes," he replied simply.

"My grandfather's arrowheads? Are you sure?" With shaking hands, she dumped them out on a small table beside her chair. She picked up a red obsidian arrowhead and looked at it carefully. "Yes! See? This little mark right here? These are his arrow heads!"

"I told you I would do everything in my power to get them back to you," he said, quietly.

"Where did you find them?" she asked with growing excitement.

"In a trash bag in the Boss' car," he said.

"Oh," she sighed. "Then you will have to hold them." Her gaze fell to them sadly.

"No, you can have them now." He smiled at her shocked look. "All the involved criminal parties in the case are deceased. These are not needed for evidence to convict anyone. We took pictures, but I got permission from the District Attorney to return them to you." There was a softness in his eyes that tugged at her heart.

She stood frozen in place, not believing her ears. This was a dream come true, these were the most important worldly possession she owned!

"Thank you!" she said, suddenly stepping forward and

standing on her tip toes. She impulsively threw her arms up to hug him and immediately retracted into herself as she gasped in pain.

"Are you alright?" he asked with concern, bending to put an arm around her waist and support her elbow with his hand. Slowly, she straightened.

"Yes, I am fine," she said, "I was just so excited and grateful, I wanted to say thank you!" she groaned. She turned her head and found her lips inches from his. Slowly, they rose together, then stood, their eyes locked. "How can I ever thank you!" she said, impulsively rising on her tip toes again and kissing him lightly on the lips.

Surprised, he slipped his arms around her and for a few seconds, they stood locked in place, their faces inches apart, and then Jeff leaned his mouth to hers, heat radiating as he breathed her in, and gently brushed his lips over hers, then sought them again for a yearning, sweet, soft kiss. She pulled back to look into his eyes, then nuzzled her lips across his tenderly. His powerful arms drew her close to him, acutely conscious of her injury while surrounding her with strength. He sought her mouth with an intensity he had never known. Her tongue explored his until they locked in an embrace mindless of the world around them, sharing a deep kiss that electrified the air with its intensity.

Sam watched for a few minutes, then grinning, walked around the other side of the house. He was planning his going away barbecue with Tom and Bodie, who had asked to bring Cheryl. He no longer worried that Jeff and Susanna would be uncomfortable around each other. In fact, the rest of them might have to retreat inside if those two kept that up. He wouldn't worry about Susanna when he went back to Afghanistan. "Stateside mission accomplished," he said aloud to himself, grinning.

24853850R00102

Made in the USA
Columbia, SC
28 August 2018